The Summer
of
Jack London

Other books by Andrew J. Fenady:

The Man With Bogart's Face
The Secret of Sam Marlow
Claws of the Eagle

The Summer
of
Jack London

A novel by

Andrew J. Fenady

**Walker and Company
New York**

First published in the United States of America in 1985 by the Walker Publishing Company, Inc.

Published simultaneously in Canada by John Wiley & Sons Canada, Limited, Rexdale, Ontario.

Library of Congress Cataloging in Publication Data

Fenady, Andrew J.
   The summer of Jack London.

   1. London, Jack, 1876–1916, in fiction, drama, poetry, etc.   I. Title.
PS3556.E477S9 1985   813'.54   84–13218
ISBN 0–8027–4040–5

Printed in the United States of America

Book Design by Teresa M. Carboni

10 9 8 7 6 5 4 3 2 1

for
ERIKA THEUKE
who was there at the beginning and
DUKE FENADY
who was there at the finish and
MARY FRANCES
who was there always

◁ CHAPTER 1 ▷

THE KILLING WAS over. The *North Star* was bound for San Francisco from the Sea of Japan. Her scuppers had run red with blood and now, keel-heavy, the eighty-ton, three-masted schooner dipped at full sail, heading due east through the trades with a fresh breeze astern and Jack London at the helm.

Able-bodied seaman Jack London, not yet twenty-one, put down a couple of spokes and felt the vessel respond and cleave the pulsing water under press of sail. His large, strong hands rested easily but firmly on the wheel. His eyes, the color of the distant sunlit sea, squinted at the vast, liquid horizon.

His face was calm and peaceful now, a handsome face with coarse, chestnut hair twining across an ample, sun-bronzed brow, a face set upon a muscle-corded neck, thick shoulders, deep chest, and heavy arms. But the voyage of the *North Star* these last months had been anything but calm and peaceful, and London knew there would be more violence ahead—the violence of nature and, with the ship under the command of Captain Erik Diequest, the violence of man.

Captain Diequest. London cast a glance at the man who stood not ten feet away looking eternally ahead, over the prow of his ship, with eyes of fire and ice, arms akimbo, a dead cigar clamped in his stone-carved jaw. He was dressed in devil's black from head to heel; a heavy, double-breasted sea jacket wrapped his huge chest, and a peaked captain's hat fit square over his forehead. Diequest feared no man, and no man defied him or even questioned him—not aboard the *North Star,* not anywhere.

Until he met Diequest, Jack had had the greatest admiration for the Vikings. Big, blue-eyed, and powerful, the Scandinavians were the best seamen in the world. But here was one Viking who, in London's book, could go to hell. He had in fact made a hell of his ship and reigned as absolutely as Lucifer himself.

Before signing on almost seven months ago, Jack London had heard stories about the infernal Norseman and his ship. Diequest had come as a child out of a bleak and desolate coast; cabin boy at twelve, ship's boy at fourteen, able seaman at seventeen—and cock of the forecastle. At twenty-one he was the master of his own ship and destiny— and master of those who, like Jack London, signed aboard the floating world of Captain Diequest.

Diequest was in his midforties now, still at the peak of his physical power. Time had not mellowed him. Time had sharpened and honed the cutting edge of the blade that carved him away from the crowd into a life of absolute rule and infinite loneliness.

But, like the rest of the crew, Jack had signed the articles and shipped with Diequest because all the other sealing schooners in San Francisco, fully crewed, had already sailed for the Bonin Islands and the Sea of Japan. Diequest's ship was always the last to leave port—and always the first to return, carrying the ghosts of countless seals and cashing in at the highest market price.

For nearly seven months, the *North Star's* crew had endured the stringent discipline, the bad food, and the abuse meted out by her master. But now, holding the helm due east, London thought of home: of his father, mother, and sister Eliza. He would bring them enough money to cover the kitchen table and laugh and get drunk, and no matter how broke in the time to come, he would never ship out with Lucifer again.

London thought, too, of the mountain of pelts stacked below, remnants of the slick and beautiful creatures who had forfeited their lives for the fancy of men and women who had never seen a living seal. He thought of the cold gray calm before the savage hunt, followed by the mass killing of the beached seals—barking rifles from the boats, wanton slaughter of the splendid dumb animals while circling seagulls watched from above Cape Jerimo.

He thought of the smell of death and of decks covered with hides and bodies, slippery with fat and blood; the scuppers streaming red; blood-splattered sails, masts, and ropes. Men, crimson of arm and hand, hard at work with ripping and flensing knives, tearing away the skins and flinging the naked carcasses to the trailing hungry sharks. And through it all, the snarling Diequest, never smiling, never satisfied, driving the crew almost, but never quite, to the point of mutiny.

London made it a practice never to speak to the captain unless Diequest spoke first. The young seaman carried out orders quickly and effectively and answered questions as tersely as possible. "Aye, sir" were the most frequently used words, spoken flat and fast.

There were those in the twenty-two-man crew who sought to curry the captain's favor, smiling obsequiously, agreeing and overagreeing with Diequest's observations about everything from the weather to whales to the White House. Politics, religion, the price of tomatoes, whatever Diequest commented on, the sycophants smiled and concurred, eagerly echoing his every comment. London noted that those who agreed most emphatically were frequently made the butt of Diequest's caprice.

Only the first mate, Cyrus Spinner, was spared. He had been with the captain for more than a dozen years and knew when to play the fool and the fox. So for seven creeping months, London did his best to avoid the captain's venom by doing more than expected and saying as little as possible.

There were times, such as now, when London knew the captain's hot-ice eyes were on him, watching and waiting for the seaman's slightest provocation, any slip of work or word. But London never slipped. In seven months at sea, before the mast and behind the wheel, London had been a sailor's sailor. But he continually reminded himself that Diequest was watching and waiting, playing the catbird's game, and there were still hundreds of miles of sea ahead before the voyage would be over.

At least his trick at the helm was over. London's replacement, John Smiley, weaved his way toward the wheel with that perpetual smile painted on his carefree face. John Smiley's original surname had long since been forgotten and supplanted by the grin that greeted friend and stranger alike. John Smiley he was called, and John Smiley he was, from San Francisco to the China Seas.

"Well, Jack, darlin', you've whistled up a happy wind and a cool breeze," he said, eyes bright and snappy. "Go below and read about Helen and the face that sunk a thousand ships."

"She's all yours, John Smiley," said London, "twelve or thirteen knots. The old girl knows how to walk."

The transfer was made without flap of sail, and London walked past Captain Erik Diequest without a word or nod. He made his way toward the forecastle, past the crewmen, most of whom seemed too old and weak to work as seamen. The oldest of the men, Smitty, struggled with two heavy buckets, then staggered and fell, his rope-thin body sprawling across the wet, salty deck.

As London lifted the old man to a sitting position, a

trickle of blood leaked from Smitty's nose. Jack removed a kerchief from his rear pocket and pressed it gently against the old man's ashen face.

"Come on, Smitty, let's get you below."

"No, Jack, thanks. Just get me to my feet . . I'm all right."

"The hell you are. Your nose is bleeding and you've got the scurvy, or I don't know wood from canvas. Come on, we're going below."

London started to lift the frail old man.

"Mr. London!" Captain Diequest's unmistakable voice split the air like a thunderclap.

London knew his time in the barrel had come.

"Aye, sir," Jack replied flat and fast.

Diequest took a single powerful step forward, as if he were preparing to leap upon a mountain. He removed the cold butt of the cigar from his wide lips and nearly broke a smile. "What is afoot, Mr. London?"

"Smitty's sick, sir. I was just helping him below."

"Is that a fact? Did your captain give an order to take Smitty below, Mr. London?"

By now the crew had ceased working and became a silent, anticipating audience. Along with London, they knew that Captain Diequest, hectoring master of his cosmos, meant to make the most of the situation. Only the ship's sounds could be heard, her hull foaming ahead, her rigging creaking.

Seaman London had finally slipped, and he knew it. The silence mounted and still Jack London did not speak.

"Answer me, Mr. London. Did your captain give an order to take that man below?"

"No, sir."

"Who is master of this vessel, Mr. London? You or me?"

"You, sir."

"I thank you for the confirmation."

"Sir," said London, "I request permission to take Seaman Smitty below—"

"Jack," Smitty whispered hoarsely. "Please . . . let it go—I'm all right."

"He's sick, sir, with the scurvy. Too sick to stand, much less work."

Diequest studied the stub of cigar between his thumb and forefinger, then looked around at the crew and let his eyes brazen back upon London. "And may I inquire," he said in mock indulgence, "from which college of medicine you graduated, *Doctor* London?"

Cyrus Spinner blustered forth his usual servile appreciation of his captain's humor. The rest of the crew remained silent.

"It doesn't take a doctor to read scurvy, sir. His gums are swollen, skin's hemorrhaging, nose is bleeding, and he's in pain if you so much as touch him . . . sir."

"I commend you on your diagnosis and suggest that you do *not* touch him." Diequest moved with light, effortless steps for a man his size until he was nearly nose to nose with London. "As a matter of fact, that is not a suggestion. It is an order."

"Then, sir, may I have your permission to take over Smitty's duties and let him go below?"

"Let's consult your patient, Dr. London. What about it, Smitty? Are you too sick to perform your duties as a member of the crew?"

"No, sir." Smitty staggered as he tried to rise. "Please, Jack, I'll be all right as soon as I get to my feet."

London reached out his right hand to help lift the old sailor to his reluctant, vinelike legs. But the instant Jack laid hand on the wavering seaman, Captain Diequest's fist, still clenching the cigar, slammed like a cannonball into London's midsection, knocking him back against the rail.

With a fighter's instinct, London started to hurl himself back toward Diequest, but his seaman's instinct prevailed. He knew the punishment for striking a captain—under any circumstances. He breathed out the hate and stared at the smirking master of the *North Star*.

"You deliberately disobeyed my order, Mr. London. I distinctly told you not to touch that man. *Didn't* I?"

"Aye, sir."

"And so the log will show." Diequest turned to Smitty, who now stood on unstable feet. "Back to your buckets, my man. Mr. Spinner, set the sky sails. There's a score of vessels too close behind. I've sworn the *North Star*'ll be the first sealer into San Francisco and, by the Almighty, she will be."

'The Almighty,' London thought to himself, Diequest is not talking about God. He's talking about himself. He is the Almighty. The Eternal. The Infinite. The Absolute. So long as they were aboard the *North Star*.

◁ CHAPTER 2 ▷

THE SEA WAS as black as the moonless night. Jack London descended into the sour, musty forecastle, a small triangular room built just under the eyes of the vessel, dimly lit by the hanging sea lamp and lined by a dozen double-tiered bunks. The walls hung heavy with oilskins, boots, and soiled garments of the sleeping seamen. The hum of their breathing formed a human chorus, accompanying the straining timbers and ghostly groans that haunted the rolling hull.

Or were they all sleeping—John Smiley, Duke Fanoudas, Beaver Blair, Oily Oily, and the rest? If not, they paid no mind to London as he maneuvered toward Smitty's bunk.

The skeletal sailor lay on his back, filmy eyes open, congealed throat breathing in hard labor with each breath. London's kerchief patted the old mariner's corrugated brow.

"Smitty. It's me, Jack."

"Who else would it be?" Smitty almost managed a smile. "Go away, Jack, you'll just get yourself in deeper trouble."

"Never mind that. Here"—London pressed something into Smitty's brittle hand—"Cookie came up with an extra potato, it'll help."

"Bless you my boy, but I've neither the grit nor the will to chew it."

"Sure you have. We'll get you home, Smitty. I swear it. We'll get your strength back."

"Strength to do what, son?"

"To live!"

"I'll have that potato, *son*," Diequest said as Spinner stood beside him, sneering at London. The captain reached down and took the potato from Smitty's infirm hand.

"Captain," said London. "It could save his life. What difference does it make to you . . ."

"What difference indeed? One more or less smelly old sailor? What value do you place on his miserable existence, against the value of this potato and all the potatoes it would take to sustain him?"

"I made a deal with Cookie—"

"I know." Diequest held up a five-dollar gold piece that Jack recognized as his own. "I know everything that goes on aboard this vessel, Mr. London. I even know what each man is thinking."

"Do you?" said London, without putting a 'sir' on it.

"Yes I do." If Captain Diequest caught the slight, he chose to ignore it. "I know what you're thinking and what the rest of these sea scum are thinking." The snoring and heavy breathing of the sailors had ceased with Captain Diequest's first words. Since those words there had been no audible breath or sound from the horizontal crewmen.

There were eight of them, including Jack and Smitty— Oily Oily, the Kanaka with smooth, black skin, salt-white teeth, and a gentle disposition except when taken advantage of; John Smiley, who smiled even in his sleep (but was he smiling now?); Duke Fanoudas, the handsome Greek, with a great black mustache, a body borrowed from his Olympic ancestors, with a hand made for the mizzen and the mandolin—a man nobody trod upon; the pathetic Hobson with his severed stump of a leg; Beaver Blair, a bloated Irishman who swore this was his last voyage, just as he'd sworn on the last dozen voyages; and Fetsui Louie, a middle-aged Chinaman, hairless and speechless, who could hear the fog roll in.

Diequest let the moment hang heavy as paste. "And this is my answer, Mr. London, to you and the rest of the crew." He closed his fingers around the potato, squashing it into a mushy mess that fell to the flooring. He wiped the pulpy remnants on the bunk beside him, turned and walked the length of the room, and climbed the companion stairs with Spinner at his heels.

The room was silent.

London looked at the cadaverous creature on the bunk. "I'm sorry, Smitty."

"You've given me somethin', Jack London," the sailor whispered. "You cared."

"Man overboard!" Oily Oily cried, and tossed a buoy over the rail. Shortly after eight bells, brave morning winds pushed the *North Star* east at fourteen knots, sweeping past the floating form of Smitty in the sea below.

"Hard down on your helm!" Jack London shouted at Cyrus Spinner, who held the wheel. And hold he did. Spinner never moved a spoke. Only his eyes moved toward Captain Diequest, who stood on the bridge.

"Down! Hard down!" London repeated as he sprang aft. Diequest moved and blocked London's path to the wheel.

"It's Smitty, sir! He can't last long down there. Turn her back!"

"Stay the course, Mr. Spinner," Diequest commanded. "Head east."

"Like hell!" London lunged and grabbed for the wheel. Diequest hit him from behind, three brutal blows to the ear, the kidney, and the nape. London fell to the deck. On his knees Jack looked aft at the drifting form.

The men aloft clung to the royal yards and watched with immobile faces. Not a soul moved or spoke during an eternal silent moment as the fading form crested, topped a wave, then disappeared in the trough. An entity resigned to his destiny, Smitty did not struggle or even swim. He was reconciled to his watery fate, and welcomed it.

A small boat could have made its way easily in such a sea, and in such a sea the *North Star* could easily have come to, if the order were given. But no such order came from the lips or conscience of Captain Erik Diequest. Diequest would not grant time to the sealers somewhere in the *North Star*'s wake.

In the distance westward, a graybeard carried Smitty to the surface as if in farewell salute, then plunged him beneath the face of the sea forever, leaving only the buoy floating behind.

London's eyes glistened as he wobbled to his feet and looked at Diequest, who puffed peacefully at his white-ashed cigar.

"You'll be called to answer for this, Captain Diequest, I swear by my eyes," said London.

"And answer I will," Diequest replied.

"When we reach port, I'm going to swear out a warrant, charge you with murder, and see you hang."

"Not ever, Mr. London. My answer and vindication is this living gale. Impossible to save the man. Am I right, Mr. Spinner?"

"Impossible, Captain," the Mate heartily agreed. "A living gale, sir. If you'd have brought her to, it would've taken the sticks out of her. You did the proper thing, sir. It was the ship or him."

"You neglect one fact, sir," said London. "I have eyes, and so does the rest of this crew."

"Then we'll put it to your shipmates." Diequest flicked the ash from his cigar. "What say you, men? Did your captain do the proper thing and save all souls aboard?" Diequest gazed at the motionless, suspended crew. "Did I do right and proper? You, Oily Oily? Beaver? Speak up, loud and clear!"

The two men hesitated, avoided London's look, then nodded in acquiescence.

"So it will be entered into the ship's log. And now, Mr. London, since you've made repeated reference to your keen eyesight, you'll do this ship a further service. Mr. Spinner . . ."

"Aye, Captain."

"Give Mr. London the high watch."

"Aye, Captain."

"He'll stay aloft until I order otherwise."

"Aye, Captain."

Diequest took the helm as Spinner shoved Jack London toward the mainmast. The one-legged Hobson looked at London with kindered eyes. Months ago, Hobson displeased the lord and master of the *North Star,* so Diequest sent him aloft. It was Christmas day, the coldest day of the year. Hobson froze to the ratlines, and when they brought him down, his leg had to be cut off. Spinner did the cutting—the same Spinner who now shoved Jack London toward the mainmast.

With each step of the ninety-foot ascent to the top of the mainmast, London's body ached and his head throbbed from the blows that Diequest had struck. Twice his vision blurred, but he kept climbing. He knew that Diequest and Spinner were watching and all eyes of the crew were on him.

The crew. From countries round the globe. Americans, Greeks, Irish, Scandinavians, and mongrels, but of the same breed. Sailors. Coarse and savage. Half brute, half human. Surviving from voyage to voyage. Port to port. Still, at some time they must have been a part of a family. Children, babies with mothers who suckled and sang to them. But somewhere they crossed over the boundary line from the family of man and became another breed. Sailors. A breed that mustn't show weakness, good grace, affection, or passion. Celibates. Sailors. Survivors. There were exceptions like Smitty, Hobson and John Smiley, but when it came to the rest, London could no more count on them than he could a candle in a cyclone.

Jack London lashed himself fast and waited. How long he would have to wait he did not know, nor would he remember. Time is measured in an orderly, organized manner. Seconds, minutes, hours, days, weeks, and months. But there is another measure of time, not orderly, not organized. When you are hurt and alone, exposed to a searing sun by day and spine-shivering wind at night. When your skin is carrion at noon and rime at midnight. When cold, slicing rain plummets into your eyes and ears and you can no longer contain the urine that bursts your bladder.

It is impossible to be orderly and organized and measure that kind of time. Parched and blistered lips by day and trembling, icy bones by dark.

Jack London remembered the old saying that your life would flash in front of you the moment before you died. It seemed to London that he would die here, ninety feet above the churning sea, but he didn't know the exact moment. Still he relived the vagrant links of his life again and again, but not in a flash. In a long agonizing vinculum that faded in and out of focus, just as London's life seemed to be fading out of focus and into infinity—a life that had begun January 12, 1876 in San Francisco.

Memories flickered in his half-conscious mind, bits and pieces, tattered shards of a human tapestry—his mother, Flora, small spectacled eyes, short brown curls, and a heart that was sometimes hard to find . . . an infant trying to sleep in a cold damp space, while Flora tried to communicate with the dead during a hundred seances in shadowy living rooms . . .

Blurred visions of wooden houses wobbled in his fevered brain, more than half a dozen before he was ten, none of them a home, but with the comfort of a gentle father John London, whose body was feebled by the ravages of work-beast labor. A man whose one love was farming but whose wife shackled him to the city with her wild, fruitless ventures while he worked to the ceaseless pounding and crashing of factory looms.

The love and attention of his older sister Liza, the sweet devotion of his wet nurse, Mammy Jenny, who suckled and cared for her sickly "white child" until he grew strong.

A boy of ten working the mean streets of a man's world, delivering papers, swamping saloons, and setting up pins in bowling alleys. . . .

And as the silent sun beat on his brow, he heard again and again the frantic beat of the looms that were destroying him, a thirteen-year-old boy, as they had destroyed his father. His only solace was the warmth and wisdom of the public library—books, books, books, and the tutelage of a librarian, the wonderful, illuminating Miss Ina Coolbrith . . . and Mr. Dodson, his high-school teacher, who sometimes smelled of whiskey but worshiped words and bequeathed that reverence to young Jack London. . . .

The cold, razorlike night rain sliced into his face and body and brought back memories of his oyster pirate days and Maimie, the girl who set his manhood juices flowing at the age of sixteen, when he owned his own boat, bought from French Frank with three hundred dollars borrowed from Mammy Jenny. Nights of danger, days of drinking, and then fellow oyster pirates lying dead with brains dripping out of bullet holes. A farewell drink with the pirates, Big George, Clam, Joe Goose, and Young Scratch Nelson, telling them he was done with the oyster bays and days. . . .

The unsteady swaying of the mainmast brought back the blur of his first sea voyage, aboard the sealer *Sophie Southerland,* a seventeen-year-old able-bodied seaman who had to prove his worth and did . . . the revulsion at the first killing of the seals . . . taking the wheel during a typhoon off the coast of Japan and holding the *Sophie Southerland* safe against the storm.

But after that, the groan and roar of the jute mill again, where an hour of his labor was worth ten cents and his mind worth nothing. . . .

Swaying ninety feet above the sea, he thought he would never walk upon dry land again as he had when he tramped the road with Kelly's Army—an army of the unemployed marching on Washington. The rods and railroad cars, hobo camps and jails. . . .

Days and nights of delusion on the mainmast, of hopelessness and hunger and the memory of his brief stint as a student at the university, a nonconformist, preferring to work and learn and write at his own pace.

And then the *North Star*. There'd been no other vessel available, no other choice; he couldn't afford the university any longer and he'd sworn he would never go back to the jungle of the jute mill—better a hell ship than that, better Captain Diequest.

So much living in so short a time. But he could not hold out much longer. So much left undone, unseen, unwritten. . . .

And then somewhere, somehow, the dreamlike recollection of hands, helping hands, firm and strong, untying him, and words, words of hope and encouragement from the mouths of John Smiley and Duke Fanoudas telling him his ordeal was over. They would get him down.

The great sails boomed like cannons and the three rows of reef-points slatted against the canvas, like a volley of rifles in salute. Jack London would live.

The next thing London knew, he was standing beside Spinner and facing Captain Diequest, who sat smoking a cigar behind an oversize teak desk.

This was the first time London had been inside the captain's quarters. The room was unlike any other captain's cabin Jack had ever seen. More like a library, its three walls were lined with books. Jack was too dizzy and weak to note the titles, but he did notice that on the captain's desk were ten or twelve books that belonged to him, books that had been stored along the wall beside his bunk. And there was a stack of papers with notes and observations that London had written about the voyage, the crew, and Captain Diequest.

"Well Mr. London, you look as if you could use a dose of sleep after your trick or two on watch—and sleep you shall, just as soon as we conclude the business at hand." Diequest turned the ship's log toward London, who was getting weaker by the moment. The captain dipped his pen into the inkwell and held it out toward Jack. "I've made the entry in the log concerning Mr. Smith. The mate has verified and signed for the officers. I thought you'd care to do the same as representative of our fine and distinguished crew—*then* you can get some sleep."

London stared with glazed eyes at Diequest. The young sailor swayed and almost fell, but Spinner's hand grabbed his shoulder and held him firm. London shook Spinner off, looked at the pen a moment, then took it.

He signed the log. Diequest immediately reached forward, retrieved the pen, spun the log back before him, blotted the signature, and closed the book.

"Very good, Mr. London. That concludes the business at hand. By the by, while you were aloft, I took the liberty of borrowing several of your books. You are in no condition to be burdened with them at this time. Why don't you come back tomorrow morning—say, six bells. Your head'll be clearer then and we might even have a little visit."

On legs of solid sponge, London made his way to his bunk. There were words of greeting and cheer from his shipmates, but it was all a scrambled blur and meant nothing. The only thing with meaning and worth at that moment was his blessed bunk. He ached for the opiate of sleep. To be alive and to be asleep. The best of both worlds. Both belonged to London. Life and slumber. Jack London plunged into the sleep of his young life.

"Come in, Mr. London."

At precisely six bells, London knocked on the heavy door of the captain's cabin and entered at Diequest's invitation.

"Yes, come in, Mr. London. Sit down. Would you like some coffee and biscuits?"

"No, sir."

"Well sit down anyhow."

London had never seen the man in so genial a mood. Jack could scarcely believe that this was the same brute who mercilessly bullied the crew for the past seven months, who sent him aloft to nearly die, and who murdered Smitty just as surely as this ship was floating.

With clearer head and vision now, London could make out some of the titles and authors of the volumes lodged in the floor-to-ceiling shelves: Bulfinch's *Age of Fable,* Johnson's *Natural History,* scientific works of Tyndall, Proctor, and Darwin, Darwin, Darwin; a number of grammars: Metcalf, Reed, Kellogg, a copy of *The Dean's English,* and, lying open on the captain's desk, Milton's *Paradise Lost.*

"A little surprised at what you see here, Mr. London?"

"More than a little."

"*Sir.*"

"Sir."

"Yes, let's not forget that the world is not made up of equals."

"Not this world, sir."

"Nor any living world. It's all the same. All a part of strength. The strong survive."

"So do the weak."

"Only at the whim of the strong."

"But not in a *civilized* world. Isn't that what makes man different from beast, sir?"

"What makes you different from the rest of this crew, Mr. London?" Diequest pointed to Jack's books, still lying on the captain's desk. "Is it these books? The knowledge you've taken from them? Is that what makes you different? What makes you better?"

"I'm no better than Smitty was, sir, but you let him die."

"He's better off as food for the fishes."

"Why didn't you let *me* die? Because of these books, sir?"

"Maybe, partly. But the point is that my will and my will alone decided that he was better off dead. Have you ever been to East London, Mr. London?"

"Not yet, sir."

"Don't go. That's the civilized world, an abyss of wretched, sodden men and women in obscene squalor, digging at garbage dumped in mud for rotten beans and potatoes, ragged children clustered like maggots around a festering mass of decayed fruit and devouring the vile rot. That's the civilized world I want no part of."

"So you made a world of your own, is that it, sir?"

"Yes. Yes, that's it."

"But why make that world a hell for the men on this ship, sir?"

"Because that's what they understand and respect—strength. Not knowledge. Not what's in the pages of these books. But the bone and muscle of these arms and shoulders—and a will of steel. Otherwise this ship would sink in a sea of insubordination, chaos, and anarchy. It's all here in Milton."

Captain Diequest tapped his strong fingers onto the open pages of *Paradise Lost.* He quoted from memory:

"Hurled into hell, he was unbeaten.
He led a lost cause and was not
afraid of God's thunderbolts. A
third of God's Angels he led with him.

. . . and in my choice to reign is
worth ambition, though in hell.
*Better to reign in hell than serve
in Heaven.*

"Don't you agree with that, Mr. London?"

London studied his captain for a moment. Diequest's face

was smooth-shaven, and every feature—brow, eyes, nose, and jaw—cut sharp and strong. With clear, cold Nordic eyes of savage beauty, his nose was Grecian, his lips full and sensual, and any woman would have prized the tawny color and flow of his soft, thick hair. He was in truth a man of physical beauty. He appeared calm and at peace with the world and himself.

In a fraction of that moment, London reprised the things he had heard about Captain Diequest, and the things he had heard and seen the captain say and do, and still here sat a calm and peaceful man with a look that was almost beatific. Not an immoral man. Unmoral.

Here is a man, thought London, one of the best sailors on God's green oceans, a man of uncommon strength and superior intelligence. He might've led an armada, an entire navy, a nation, but instead he squashed a potato and doomed a harmless old sailor.

"Captain," Jack responded, "I've learned to agree with everything you say aboard this ship. Do I get my books back?"

"You do. Mostly fiction, I see. Kipling, Melville, Flaubert, Maupassant. Yes, go ahead and take them."

"And my notes?"

"Yes. I see you've written a lot about the sailors and the seals, but not very much about me."

"I didn't know you very well, Captain."

"Well, you know me better now, don't you?"

"Yes, sir, I do."

"I've enjoyed our little visit, Mr. London. I don't have anybody to talk to except Spinner, and while he's loyal, he's not exactly a literary man."

London rose and collected his books and notes from Diequest's desk. The Captain obviously hadn't found the sheaf of papers Jack had secreted in the bulkhead by his bunk, the papers that delt in detail with Captain Erik Diequest.

London had made up his mind that once again he would be a sailor's sailor. He would give Captain Diequest no cause for conflict again. Whenever any of the crew mumbled discontent, Jack London walked away. He would stand his watch and take his turn at the wheel. When addressed by Diequest, "Aye, sir" would be his only reply. He would serve his time in hell, and he would survive—if not prevail.

Seaman Jack London was the first of the watch on deck and the last to drop below. He had four legs and six hands and never left a sheet or tackle for a shipmate to coil over a pin. He made music when he worked, the sweet music of life and youth and hope. And when he wasn't working, he wrote. A thousand, two thousand words a day or night. Every detail of the voyage—every insult and transgression, every infraction, every violation, every crime committed by the master of the *North Star* and his mate—was duly recorded by London, and the documentation secreted in the safety of the unsuspected bulkhead.

But despite all his will and discipline, Jack London would not reach shore without incident.

Cookie was the cause. Actually it was Diequest, but London didn't know it at the time. Cookie, Archie Billingsgate, the ship's cook, was a fugitive from the Middle Ages, as scummy as the pots and kettles in his greasy kitchen, and smelling of sour sweat and cheap, sweet cooking wine. That day Cookie was on a mission, and he meant to get his due. He did.

Jack London had just set a skysail. His feet barely touched the deck when he was accosted by Cookie, while crew and officers looked on. "You bloody bastard, you owe me five dollars gold. Pay now!"

London knew it was no joke. Humor was not a part of Cookie's way of life, but the knife with seven inches of Swiss steel glistening within the strings of his dirty apron was.

"We made a bargain and I kept my part. *Potatoes!* Now

you pay me the five dollars gold you promised," he slurred, with the smell of sweet wine on his breath, "or I'll rip you from belly to brisket."

Cookie pulled the knife from the apron and pointed it toward Jack's breastbone. Jack knew another moment might be too late. His left hand grasped Cookie's wrist and pounded it against the mast, while his right fist crashed full force into Cookie's nose, splintering bone and cartilage and flushing blood down the mouth and neck of the stunned giant.

But Cookie didn't drop the knife. His hand broke free of London's grip, and the blade arched upward, ready to plunge into Jack's throat, but not before the young sailor hit Cookie again and again with relentless savagery, until Cookie dropped senseless to the deck.

London reached down, tore the knife from Cookie's grasp, struck the point hard into the deck, and snapped off the blade halfway to the hilt.

"Throw a bucket of water over him." Diequest's voice boomed the order to John Smiley. "That'll be the closest he's come to washing since we left California." The Captain's heavy hand pounded London's shoulder in a congratulatory clap. "Well, my man, you've made soup of him, sure enough." Diequest led London toward the rail as John Smiley threw a second bucket of salt water over Cookie, and the rest of the crew went back to work, commenting favorably on the outcome of the confrontation.

"Why did he come after me for the gold piece?" London pressed both knuckles against the rail. "You took it from him, he knew you had it?"

"Because I told him I gave it back to you and it was his to keep if he could get it." Diequest smiled.

London turned and faced the captain. "Why?"

"To see what would happen," Diequest said. "To give truth to my credo. The strong survive."

"Either one of us could've been killed."

"That was your lookout."

"Just for your amusement—"

"Yes. You see, you were stronger so you smashed him. Right or wrong is of no significance, justice of no importance, merit of no consequence. The only thing that matters is strength. That's the only thing that ever matters."

"Aboard this ship, sir."

"*Anyplace.*"

"I'm happy, sir," London breathed deeply, "that we were able to provide you with some amusement."

"Yes," Diequest replied, walking away, "so am I."

That night in his bunk, Jack London wrote about the events of the day and his conversation at the rail with Captain Diequest. On the far side of the forecastle, Duke Fanoudas played a melody on his mandolin while John Smiley sang again the words he had sung ten thousand times during his life at sea, the words of "The Song of the Trade Wind."

"Oh, I am the wind the seamen love—
  I am steady, and strong, and true;
They follow my track by the clouds above,
  O'er the fathomless tropic blue.

Through daylight and dark I follow the bark,
  I keep like a hound on her trail;
I'm strongest at noon, yet under the moon,
  I stiffen the bunt of her sail."

Sailors, Jack London thought to himself, their home is everywhere—and nowhere. He finished writing the final entry into his journal of the ship's voyage. Tomorrow the *North Star* would be back in San Francisco.

◁ CHAPTER 3 ▷

SAN FRANCISCO—THE Athens of America, a sobriquet used unsparingly by the citizens of that city, those citizens who knew there was an Athens.

San Francisco—the cool gray city, gateway to the Orient, Alaska, Australia, and the South Pacific, with enough room around the bay's four hundred seventy-five square miles to berth every ship afloat on the seas.

San Francisco—the largest natural harbor in the world. Spanish and English galleons had sailed past the Golden Gate as early as the sixteenth and seventeenth centuries, unaware of the fog-shrouded bay until 1775, when Captain Don Manuel Ayala, lost in the fog, steered his Spanish packet *San Carlos* into the bay and spent weeks surveying his wondrous find before sailing out again to spread word of his discovery to all the world.

Within a year, Captain Juan Bautista de Anza brought a boatload of settlers and named the colony Yerba Buena because of the blanket of green mint that covered the hillsides. The two hundred inhabitants raised sheep and cattle and families until 1846, when the U.S. Naval vessel *Portsmouth,* under the command of Commander John Montgomery, landed an armed contingent ashore, raised the American flag and proclaimed the territory a possession of the United States. The Spaniards were in no position to decline the honor.

In 1847 the town council officially named the village of four hundred fifty persons San Francisco, and within a year the population doubled.

Then James Marshal found a glittering substance at Sutter's Mill and unleashed a stampede of 'forty-niners, who swelled the city to twenty five thousand seekers of fortune.

For the next fifty years, countless fortunes were made and lost, not just in gold, but in shipping, fishing, canning, railroading, land development, and "speculation," which translated to almost anything that would turn a profit. Italians, Greeks, Chinese, Scandinavians, Irish, English and all breeds from all points of the compass crammed into the beautiful bay area.

The rich rose to the top of Nob Hill. Stanford, Spreckeles, Tobin, Towne, Flood, Hopkins, Colton, Crocker, and the others looked down from their magnificent mansions on the masses who took up space below.

It was a city of sables and socialists, Bernhardt and the Barbary Coast, Cliff House and Chinatown, the Tivoli and Tong Wars, Isadora Duncan and "Deadman's Alley," champagne and Shipwreck Kelly, opera and opium, High Society and Sodom and Gomorrah.

It was a literary garden, where people of letters lived and visited: Ambrose Bierce, Gertrude Atherton, Frank Norris, Robert Louis Stevenson, Brete Harte, Mark Twain, and Rudyard Kipling, who observed: "San Francisco is a mad city inhabited by perfectly insane people whose women are of a remarkable beauty."

The *North Star* was docked in a slip south of the Ferry Terminal, at the foot of Market Street. Her keel floated high in the water, her canvas folded, cargo unloaded and sold to Herman Leebes Company, and her crew was being paid off and was debarking.

As Captain Diequest smoked his cigar, Spinner called the

sailors' names, and the paymaster seated behind the table on the deck traded money for each seaman's signature or mark on the book before him.

"Fanoudas," Spinner called out. The big Greek stepped forward, signed the book, stuffed the money into his pocket, hoisted his seabag over his shoulder and walked past Diequest without exchanging a look or a word.

"Hobson," Spinner intoned. The sailor with the crude facsimile of a wooden leg made his way to the table and received his compensation for the voyage, which included the loss of his left leg. He hobbled wordlessly past Captain Diequest, who puffed pleasantly and inhaled the cigar smoke.

"London," Spinner sang out, and Jack took his turn at the table, signed and collected, then shouldered his seabag and walked toward Diequest.

"Mr. London." It was the first time Captain Diequest had spoken to any of the departing crew.

"Aye, sir."

"Did we furnish you with sufficient material for your literary endeavors?"

"Yes, *sir.*"

"Good. We wouldn't want to disappoint the next Rudyard Kipling."

Spinner made a point of laughing with forced gusto as London moved on.

"Once we came to terms," Diequest continued, "you were as good a seaman as I had on board. You're welcome to ship with me again."

"Thank you, sir," said London as he caught up to Hobson, who was having difficulty negotiating the gangplank that led to the dock.

"Here, Hobby," said Jack, "let me give you a hand."

"It's not a hand I need, lad. It's a leg," Hobson replied. "But thanks."

When London and Hobson set foot on land, Jack turned back and faced the *North Star*.

"Captain Diequest, sir."

"Yes, Mr. London," Diequest puffed from the rail.

"Just one thing more, Captain, *sir*. You can go straight to hell."

The crew on and off the ship stiffened. Captain Diequest held his look on London.

"This distance is deceiving to the ears, Mr. London. Would you come closer and repeat what you just said?"

"This is dry land I'm standing on, not your ship. You want to hear better, *you* come closer."

A wave of excitement galvanized the crew and dock hands. No man had ever spoken in such manner to Captain Diequest.

The master of the *North Star* brushed by Cyrus Spinner and walked with unhurried strides down the gangplank. The men on the dock formed an arc that became an arena as Diequest stopped within arm's length of Jack London.

"So you reason that down here I'm not your captain, London? Down here we're equals, is that it?"

"I value myself above being the equal of a wanton murderer."

"Maybe you'd want to put a voice to your complaints, so all your mates can hear." Diequest tossed away the cigar. "Before I tear the tongue out of your face."

"I've done more than that. I've put it on paper. Names and dates, all documented."

Diequest nodded and grinned at the crewmen. "Our ship's log isn't good enough for Mr. London. He keeps one of his own."

"All written down." London spat out the words. "How you pocket the food money and ladle up slop, how you goad the men into fighting each other for your amusement and clap 'em in the lazarette if they look at you sideways, how you bullied Hobson aloft in a storm and let him freeze to the ratlines till his leg had to come off, how you let old Smitty die, murdered him just as sure as—"

"It makes for fine literature, doesn't it? And now I'll put the final entry in your book myself." As he spoke, Captain Diequest whipped his hugely knuckled fist at London.

But Jack swung the seabag in front of him and let it absorb the blow as it dropped. He crashed a hook into Diequest's ear and pressed with a wild whirlwind of lefts and rights, but Diequest would not go down. His stone fist cracked against London's cheekbone, then the bigger man threw his bearlike arms around Jack's body, and thrust them both to the ground.

Later London would write in his journal: *We fell upon each other like bulls . . . with fists, with hatred, with desire to hurt, maim, destroy. All the painful thousand years climb through creation . . . lost. Two savages of the stone age, of the squatting place and the tree refuge . . . sinking lower and lower, back into the dregs of the new beginnings of life, colliding, recoiling and colliding again and eternally again.*

Until London stood weaving, pumping the expired air into his burning lungs and Diequest, for the first time in his life, lay in a bloodied, crumpled, unconscious heap.

All the spectators and sailors on ship and dock—all but Spinner and Cookie—cheered and waved their approval at the outcome. The first mate and the cook retrieved their fallen captain and carried him up the gangplank onto the *North Star.*

The other seamen wanted to buy Jack drinks and together savor his victory for all of them. But Jack begged off. He walked to a faucet, turned it on, and scooped handfuls of water onto his bruised face. Duke Fanoudas brought over Jack's seabag.

Jack London hefted it onto his shoulder, waved farewell to his shipmates, and walked away from the *North Star.*

As he stood on his leg and stump and watched the victorious young sailor move off, tears dropped down the face of Hobson.

◁ CHAPTER 4 ▷

JACK LONDON WOULD board one more ship before his voyage home ended. He took the ferry steamer *Solano* across the bay and landed in Oakland. And there would be one more stop before he crossed the threshold to home and family.

London stood at Twelfth and Jefferson Streets in front of Oakland High School, where he had attended but not graduated. Not much had changed; there was a fist fight going on in the school yard. A battalion of students cheered and jeered at two of their classmates, who were pommeling each other, falling down, rolling over, rising again and again, and engaging in a less effective and far less brutal version of the fight between London and Diequest at the dock. Still there were bruises and blood.

London watched a minute or more before carrying his seabag through the circle of young spectators toward the combatants, who were on the ground again.

"All right, mates," said Jack. "Break it up."

The gladiators ignored his suggestion, and the onlookers vocalized their displeasure at the would-be peacemaker.

"Mind your own beeswax!"

"Ship out, sailor!"

"Leave 'em be!"

"Who asked youse?"

London smiled, set his seabag on the ground, reached down, grabbed the scrawny warriors, and pulled them apart.

"That'll do, fellas." Jack held a firm grip on each of the boys. "Let's call it a draw."

The crowd protested the decision.

"Now, men." London adopted an avuncular tone. "Don't you fellas know that—"

The taller, duskier campaigner sucker-punched the smaller, redhead fighter.

"Here! Stow that!" London rattled the puncher. "Don't you know that fighting is the debate of the ignorant?"

"Yeah?" The redhead pointed to Jack's bruised face. "How'd you get that?"

"What's your name, boy?" London grinned.

"Dolan. What's yours?"

"London."

"Geez!" Dolan exclaimed. "Are you Jack London?"

"Guilty," said Jack, releasing his hold on the boys.

"Hey, this here's Jack London," one of the students hollered in case the others hadn't heard.

"I thought he was older," somebody said.

"I thought he was bigger," another added.

"My name's Martinez." The dusky fighter beamed, extending his hand. "We know all about you."

"You do?" Jack put his palm into Martinez's. "How come?"

"Ol' man Dodson, he talks about you a whole lot."

"Yeah? What does he say?"

"He says you been a tramp," Dolan declaimed.

"Please—'on the road.' " Jack grinned.

"And you been to sea," another student chimed in. "And you're a writer."

"Mr. Dodson said that?" London thumbed his chin.

"He said you won a writing contest in the newspaper when you was seventeen."

"First and last time I was published. Twenty-five dollars for two thousand words."

" 'Typhoon Off the Coast of Japan,' " said Dolan. "We even read it in class."

"Is that so?"

"*I'm* gonna be a sailor," Dolan announced.

"Finish school first." London smiled.

"Did *you?*" Dolan smiled back.

"Let's just say my formal education's been temporarily interrupted." Jack ruffled Dolan's hair. "Now how about you two fellas shaking hands?"

"Sure," said Dolan.

"Okay, Jack." Martinez agreed, and the two boys shook.

The affair was concluded, and the students started to disperse.

"Hey, mate," Jack said to Dolan.

The redheaded youngster stood looking at London, who took up a fighter's stance.

"Keep your left hand high and your chin low."

"You bet I will, Jack." Dolan turned and started to leave.

London booted him lightly in the rear and winked. "And protect your stern at all times."

Elmer Dodson sat behind his desk in the empty classroom. The *North Star* writings of his former pupil, Jack London, were in front of him. Dodson took a swig of rye from a pint bottle, corked it, and dropped the bottle into a desk drawer, then smacked the drawer shut.

London stood near a window and listened as the old man continued to read aloud:

"By now the hunter Stacey was more dead than alive, choking in his own blood from the beating the 'Moaner' had given him. As a final act of victory, the 'Moaner' clamped his teeth into Stacey's ear and tore it from the poor man's head.

"All the time Captain Diequest watched as the decadent rulers of Rome must have watched. Then he spat his dead cigar onto the deck and turned away. It was at Diequest's whim that the two men fought.

"The *North Star* is the world we live in. Captain Diequest is the absolute ruler of that world. He rules it absolutely."

Dodson looked up at London and shook his head. He pulled open the drawer, uncorked the bottle, and downed another mouthful of rye. He ran his long bony fingers through the silvery strings of hair that had fallen across his large angular brow. He lifted the steel-rimmed glasses from his nose and let them ride on his forehead. As was his habit, Mr. Dodson rubbed his thumb and forefinger on the heavy gold chain that ran across his vest to the gold Waltham watch resting in his pocket.

"You think it's no good," London said.

"It's not your writing, Jack," Dodson shook his head again. "Oh, it's poetic, crudely poetic, and needs discipline, but that's not what I'm talking about."

"What, then?"

"The subject matter, man. Blood and biting and death."

"But it happened!"

"Who cares, Jack? Who the hell cares?"

"The men on that ship."

"They're not going to buy your stuff."

"The way you sound, *nobody* is."

"Jack, you've got to be practical. If you're ever going to make a living from writing—and damn few do—you've got to write for the marketplace, and there's no market for misery, for cruelty and death."

"Mr. Dodson"—Jack came closer to the desk—"you once told me I should write about the romance of things."

"I did."

"Well, at first I thought there was nothing but cruelty and

death on the *North Star*. But underneath, there *was* a kind of romance—in the way the sail took the wind, in the seals we were hunting, in the names of the places, in the hopes, even the tragedies, of each crewman. That's the kind of romance I want to write about!"

"Jack—"

"I want to write about things as they are—"

"Jack—"

"Not some phony, formal drawing-room kind of world full of bangles and bonbons."

"Jack—"

"I don't want to sit snug and warm and safe in some reference library and write fantasies while I get old and soft."

"Old? You're not even twenty-one!"

"You remember that poem you read to us by Walter Scott?"

"*Sir* Walter Scott. 'The Clarion'?"

"That's it. 'The Clarion.' " Jack repeated the words of the quatrain from memory:

"Sound, sound the Clarion, fill the fife!
   To all the sensual world proclaim,
One crowded hour of glorious life
   Is worth an age without a name.

"That's what I'm talking about—crowding every hour of life with glory and drama, with excitement. I want to excite people and be excited myself."

"Jack"—Dodson rapped his knuckles on London's papers—"this is not the style of stuff that sells."

"Styles change. Mr. Dodson, I know I need literary discipline—"

"Not just *literary*." Dodson smiled.

"You helped me in the beginning."

"You're the best student I ever had. You made it, well . . ." Dodson took another pull of rye. "You made it worthwhile."

"Thank you, sir." Jack leaned eagerly with both palms on the desk. "Will you help me again, Mr. Dodson?"

"How?"

"I'm going to make a novel out of this diary."

Dodson rose and scratched at his head. "Oh, now you've graduated to novels."

"I'm going to write about that wolf—Diequest—and what happened on the *North Star*. What do you say to that?"

"I say, if you've made up your mind, there's no power on land or sea that can deter you. What do you want me to do?"

"Will you read it and make suggestions?"

"I might." Dodson laughed. "Will you pay any attention to what I suggest?"

"I might." London also laughed.

Jack had known Mr. Dodson for nearly a half dozen years, and while the older man had a keen sense of humor, the two of them had not often laughed together.

Dodson was a solitary man who kept mostly to himself, his books, and his bottle. Through the years he had come close to losing his teaching position in Oakland on several occasions. There were those in authority who complained that he was not a churchgoer, not a voter, that he drank to excess and did not participate in the community's social activities as was expected of any ordinary high-school teacher. Mr. Dodson was anything but ordinary.

It was Miss Ina Coolbrith at the Oakland library who had opened the world of books to young Jack London. She hadn't exactly taught him how to read, but she had taught him what to read, and how to organize and direct his voracious energy and capacity, rather than assail the bookshelves in a hit or miss attack.

But it was Mr. Dodson who'd taught Jack how to write, if

writing can be taught. It was Mr. Dodson who encouraged the young man to set words down on paper.

"You can only learn to write by writing. Write every day. Write about what you *see*—a flower, a snake, a snail, a sunset. Write it down. Describe it. Write about what you *smell,* that same flower, the grass, supper on the stove, the inside of a church if you go there, a saloon, a boat—put it down. Write about what you feel—pain, love, hate, anger, anguish. Force yourself to write every day until it becomes a habit. Until you wouldn't think of *not* writing. Write what you see, what you smell, what you hear, what you feel, what you *live.* Put it all into words and set it down on paper. Bring it to me and I'll put it into proper grammar with subject, predicate, and object until you get the hang of it.

"Jack, where you got it I don't know. I don't know your mother or father, but somehow you have a natural bent for writing, a gift. You have got to shape and hone and polish that gift, and I'll do all I can to help you."

And help he did. While Jack was in high school, while he oyster-pirated, when he was at sea or on the road, or even at the jute mill, Jack London wrote every day and either sent or brought the pages to Mr. Dodson, who went over every page, every line, every word with his pupil.

And now writing was a habit, a drug. Jack could not think of doing without it. He could not think of *not* writing.

In spite of all their time together, Jack knew relatively little about his teacher. The most he ever learned was on a night a few years ago after Jack left school and became an oyster pirate.

The weather was foul that night, too foul to raid the oyster beds. Maimie stayed aboard the *Razzle Dazzle,* and Jack went to the First and Last Chance Saloon to hoist a few with Johnny Heinhold, the proprietor of the establishment, and play a game of chess.

It was also Dodson's habit to drop in at the Last Chance for an occasional chess game with Johnny H. and also hoist a few. On this occasion Dodson had hoisted a few too many and was asleep in a booth.

Pete Holt, a former student of Dodson's whom the teacher had repeatedly failed with just cause, thought he'd have some great sport with the unconscious academician; Holt lit a cherry bomb and put it into Dodson's breast pocket.

Jack London entered the Last Chance just in time for the explosion and the gales of laughter and knee-slapping from Holt, who boasted and bragged to everybody about his great joke. Jack hit Holt just hard enough to send the prankster, minus two front teeth, flying over a poker table and into a dark corner.

London helped the dazed teacher to his feet and took him to the *Razzle Dazzle* for repairs.

While Maimie watched, Jack applied salve and then a bandage to Dodson's scrawny chest and shoulder.

"The dirty bastard," Dodson growled as he downed half a tumbler of Jack's whiskey. "I don't mind the damage to what's left of this old bag of bones, but the son of a bitch blew apart my best jacket and clean, silk shirt—just so the bastard didn't blow up my gold-filled pocket watch." Dodson put the timepiece up to his ear. "It's still ticking, and I guess I am, too—knocked out two of his teeth, did you, boy?"

"I guess I did. Here, put on this sweater, Mr. Dodson."

"I am unalterably opposed to violence, mind you," said the old man, pulling on the sweater. "But in this case I alter my opposition and wish you had knocked out a couple more molars—who is that earthy vision of loveliness?"

"This is Maimie, Mr. Dodson."

"An honor, my lady."

"Thanks, professor, but I'm no lady. I just live here with Jack on the *Razzle Dazzle*—don't know exactly what that makes me."

"A refreshingly honest as well as dazzlingly beautiful

young lady. Jack, did I ever tell you about my beautiful young lady?" Dodson was still far from sober.

"No, sir."

"No, I haven't told anyone." Dodson poured himself another drink and spoke slowly. "It was a lot of liquor ago. I met her in college. It took me months to get up enough courage to speak to her. Her family was wealthy, bankers, and I . . . I was a poor, struggling would-be writer, but we fell in love. Her parents objected. They had plans for her—a marriage, actually a merger with another banking family. She wanted to run away with me, but I said no. She married the banker and died of pneumonia six months later. Maybe she would have died anyhow—but at least we would've had those six months together."

Dodson put his head back on the bunk, closed his eyes, then spoke again:

"I am tired of tears and laughter,
 And men that laugh and weep;
Of what may come hereafter
 For men that sow to reap;
I am weary of days and hours,
Blown buds of barren flowers
Desires and dreams and powers
 And everything but sleep. . . ."

Dodson was asleep.

"What was all that?" Maimie asked.

"It was part of a poem, by a man named Swinburne."

Neither Jack nor Dodson ever spoke of that night again.

Dodson lowered the eyeglasses from his brow back to the bridge of his nose. "How's your family, Jack?"

"Don't know. Haven't seen 'em yet." London placed his fingertips upon his bruised face. "Say, Mr. Dodson, how do I uh . . how do I look?"

◁ CHAPTER 5 ▷

"**J**ACK, DARLING, YOU look beautiful." Eliza London pressed the palms of both hands on his ears and kissed her brother on the lips and cheek.

She was eight years older than Jack, more like a mother than a sister, plain-featured but with warm brown eyes and a warmer smile on thin, pink lips. Eliza looked years older than she had when Jack left. She was not yet thirty but had the worn look of a middle-aged woman. But at the sight of her young, strong brother, she seemed suddenly younger and stronger.

Eliza threw both arms around him and hugged tightly, London winced.

"What's the matter, Jack?"

"Couple of uh . . . just a couple sore ribs."

"He *looks* like he's been fighting and drinking," Flora London said as she continued slicing vegetables atop a chopping block in the small, cluttered kitchen.

"Mom, I haven't hoisted a drink since Yokohama." London moved to kiss his mother, but she pushed him off with an elbow and a "humph."

Flora London was a petite, severe woman with a faint scar that ran across her right eyebrow—a woman of strong will and fiber. She held herself erect and seldom displayed emotion. A restless, nervous woman, she was the buckle of the London family belt. She dominated the house and those who lived in it. The house was a tiny, five-room, two-story wooden building in need of paint and lacking many shingles on the roof. It was located on Sixteenth Street and Twentieth Avenue in Oakland. The inhabitants included Flora, her husband John, Eliza, and occasionally Jack.

London had been home only a few minutes, and already he could feel the pressure of his mother's oppressiveness, her lack of humor. Jack picked up a carrot from the chopping block and swiped it across his sister's backside.

"Liza, why isn't a good-looking girl like you married yet?"

"Your sister's too damn choosy," Flora spurted. "That's why!"

"I'm waiting for somebody like you, Jack." Eliza laughed. "But nobody fills the bill."

"And what's wrong with Bernard Higginbotham, I'd like to know?" Flora exclaimed. "He owns his own grocery store, doesn't drink or smoke, and is getting pretty damn tired of asking Miss Uppity here to marry him. He'll find someone younger and prettier before long, and then you'll end up being Miss Sorry, Liza London."

"Bernard Higginbotham is a musty, miserly old man who smells like rotten cheese," said Jack, and took a bite out of the carrot.

"He does at that." Eliza laughed again. "And all he wants is a housekeeper and someone to help with the store, and he's close to fifty, maybe even past."

"Well, your father was no colt when I married him." Flora whacked a head of cabbage in half.

"Say, where is Dad?" Jack asked. "Is he working?"

"Like hell," Flora grunted. "He's out for a walk. He'll never be fit to work again. And do you know how far in debt we are? How much I've had to borrow?"

"Oh no, we're not. Pay it all back!" Jack pulled out a roll and spread it over the kitchen table. "Home is the sailor . . .

with a bundle. We've got almost three hundred dollars in the kip."

"Three hundred?" Flora's eyes widened.

"The *North Star* was first into port and payed off high, wide, and handsome."

"Well"—Flora reverted to her usual expedient self—"That won't last long. Have you thought about what you're going to do next?"

"Nope." Jack finished off the carrot.

"You're not going to ship out again, are you Jack?" Eliza asked.

"No, sweet sister, this bird is home for the summer."

"Maybe you can get on at the jute mill," Flora suggested, still slicing at the cabbage. "Mrs. Kennedy said they might—"

"I'll not be a work beast again, Mom! Not for ten cents an hour, twelve hours a day, not Jack London!"

"And just what are your plans, *Mister* London?"

"*Mister* London is going to do some writing, some relaxing, and some thinking. Get back my land legs, and after that—" Jack stopped as he caught sight of his father opening the back door. It was not a pleasant sight.

John London seemed to be functioning by rote, and not very well. He was gaunt, a bent and beaten white-haired man who plodded along with the aid of a cane.

Jack rushed to embrace him.

"Dad! How are you, you old tiger? Hey, you're getting pretty fancy these days with that walking stick." Jack's arms swept around the old man. He was shocked at how brittle and bloodless his father felt.

"Jack, my boy . . ." Tears welled from the old man's vacant eyes. "I prayed, I prayed that you'd be . . . that I'd still be . . ." The cane fell from the old man's hand. Jack quickly reached down, retrieved the stick, and guided his father toward a kitchen chair.

"Here, Dad. Come on over and sit down."

"Better take him to his room, out of the way," Flora said without looking up from her chopping. "He'll need to rest before supper."

London looked at Flora. He started to say something but held up. He thought to himself, not a word of welcome, or greeting, or warmth. Not a smile or gesture. Just chop, chop, chop, and get the old man out of the way. The old man. His father. Her husband, who had worked like a dray horse year after year, moving from house to house and job to job at Flora's whim. Trying every task, unhappy at everything except farming, the one thing he knew and loved, but which displeased Flora London. Grinding away at mill and mine until he himself was ground away.

Yes, Mom, Jack thought to himself, better take him to his room, out of the way. He'll need to rest . . . he'll need more than rest, but I'll take him to his room. Out of the way.

Jack led his father into the bedroom and started to help him toward the bed.

"No, Jack." John London motioned in the direction of the rocking chair near the window. "The chair, the chair will be fine."

Jack guided his father's frail body into the chair and covered the old man's legs with a quilt. He knelt before him and took both his father's cold, thin hands into his own. John London turned his face away and wept.

"Dad. Dad, you're going to be all right . . ."

"I didn't . . . want to be like this."

"Come on, everybody's got a right to be sick once in a while. But not too long, mind you."

"I just wanted to see you again—"

"See me! Hell, we'll go to the Tivoli together . . . and down to Johnny H's. I'll take you sailing and fishing, and we're going to plant a little garden out back and grow the fattest, reddest tomatoes in Oakland. How does that sound?"

"It sounds good, Jack. And it sounds good to hear your

voice, young and strong. I'll need some of your strength. I'll get better now that you're back."

"You bet you will."

"Jack, your mother, she, well . . . she doesn't mean to be . . . like she seems, but it hasn't been easy for her, 'specially these last months while you were away, and I've been sick . . ."

"I know, Dad."

"And, I . . . I haven't been a husband—you understand?"

Jack London looked into the empty gaze in his father's eyes, eyes without hope or purpose, eyes of ache and dread and suffering, of waste and despair. Only a few years ago this had been a strong and virile man.

Was this a prophecy? A portent? A mirror? Were these Jack London's eyes thirty or forty years from now? Time's tragedy? Was he his father's son? Was this the shape of things to be?

John London breathed deeply and closed his tired eyes. "I think I'll just . . . now that you're here, I think I'll just rest awhile."

"You do that, Dad. Take a little rest." Jack rose and walked to the door. He looked at the frail old man who sat motionless in the rocking chair against the afternoon light by the window, then Jack London turned and closed the door behind him.

In the kitchen, Flora was still chopping and Eliza was shelling peas.

"He looks terrible," Jack said softly. "What's wrong with him?"

"What isn't?" Flora replied, chop, chop, chopping.

"Have you taken him to a doctor?"

"Yes, Jack," Eliza answered, "we've taken him. The doctor gave him medicine, but there's no medicine that can cure him. His heart is weak and he's just plain worn out."

"Just like the machines at the mill. When they wear out,

toss 'em on the ash heap and replace 'em. But how do you replace a father . . . or a husband?"

"Everybody gets old and dies, Jack," Flora said.

"Well, let's not bury him yet, Mom." Jack walked to the window, looked out a moment, then turned with a change of attitude. "As a matter of fact, I've got a pip of an idea! Let's all go out to supper tonight. Maybe—"

"Supper's on the stove," Flora said, dimming the bright look that had shot into Eliza's eyes.

"Won't it keep until tomorrow?" Jack asked.

"It already has." Flora dumped the chopped vegetables into the iron kettle on the stove. "I'm just freshening it up. Besides, don't you want some good home cooking after eating the garbage they serve on that boat?"

"*Ship*, Mom, not boat. And I guess I could use some good home cooking, but maybe after supper we can all go out and—"

"After supper we're having a seance," Flora announced.

"A *seance!*" Jack laughed. "Mom, are you still—"

"Still what?" Flora was not amused. "It's a proven fact that we can communicate with the dead. I've done it many times."

"Okay."

"And we're going to do it tonight. Charlie and Mabel Krugheimer are coming over, and so is Maurice Duvier. His wife passed away on Easter Sunday and we're going to call her back tonight. You're welcome to sit in if you think you can—"

"Uh . . . no, Mom, thanks." Jack looked at Eliza, who did her best to repress a smile. "I think I'll go out and communicate with the living."

"Since when is drinking and brawling considered communicating?" Flora inquired.

"Drink? Brawl? Me? Never! Mom, you must be thinking of your other son." Jack smiled.

"Thank God I haven't got another son." Flora stirred the kettle. "One's enough to send me to an early grave."

"Don't worry, Mom, you won't be sent for, not for a long, long time. Say, I've got presents for everybody soon as I unpack. And for me . . ." Jack picked up a ten-dollar bill from the kitchen table.

Flora ceased her stirring and looked at her son.

"For me, a new secondhand suit, a couple shirts, rent for a typewriter, and just a few beers." Jack winked. "Give my regards to the ghosts."

◁ CHAPTER 6 ▷

JACK LONDON PULLED away the clean white sheet that had just been hung on the line with the freshly laundered towels and clothes.

"Mammy Jenny!" He grinned.

"Johnny, my baby! Johnny!!" The big, handsome black woman's face was aglow. She threw her arms around him and hugged him to her breast. These were the arms that cared for him as a baby, and this was the breast that nursed him when Flora was unable to nourish her infant.

Mrs. Jenny Prentiss, who lived down the road, had lost her own son at birth and became wet nurse to Jack London—and more, much more. Jack took the place of her stillborn child, and she heaped upon him all the attention, affection, and love that Flora was unwilling or incapable of giving.

Mammy Jenny nourished him physically and spiritually. She sang him lullabies, cleaned and cuddled and powdered her surrogate son, and provided all the strength, warmth, and security that was lacking in Flora's mechanism.

When sixteen-year-old Jack London decided to strike out on the dangerous adventure path of oyster-pirating, it was to Mammy Jenny he came for a loan of three hundred dollars; And he got what he came for, in shiny twenty-dollar gold pieces, saved by the ex-slave from her work as a nurse at the hospital.

And now, in the backyard of her immaculate cottage, she cried with happiness as she hugged and kissed her son who had come back from the sea again.

"Johnny! Johnny, let me look at you! These tired old eyes haven't seen anything so beautiful in a long time. I thought you were on the other side of the world!"

"I was."

"And you were in my prayers every day and night." She touched his face. "Johnny, you been fighting?"

"Would you believe me"—Jack laughed—"if I said I ran into a door?"

"Looks like that door had a kick like a mule. Did you win, Johnny?"

"I won, Mammy Jenny."

"Good! Come on in and I'll fix you something to eat."

"No thanks, I'm on the run."

"You running from trouble or toward it?"

"Neither, Mammy Jenny." Jack produced a small, plainly wrapped package from under his jacket. "Here's a present . . . from the other side of the world." Jack had bought a pipe for his father and silk shawls for Flora, Eliza, and Mammy Jenny. He placed the package in her hands.

"Thank you, baby." She was still tearful with happiness. "You need anything?"

"I know where to come if I do." Jack kissed her and turned away.

"God bless you, Johnny."

"Don't work so hard," Jack called back as he vaulted over the picket fence.

"I hear you," Mammy Jenny replied.

◁ CHAPTER 7 ▷

THERE WAS AN old Oliver typewriter on the barroom table, along with a bundle wrapped in newspaper and tied by string, an empty beer pitcher, and two empty glasses. Also on the table there were the elbows of two men locked in an arm-wrestling contest. One of the arms belonged to Jack London, who wore his new-used suit, the other to a bull of a sailor, Leach Davits.

The Hatch was one of the many saloons located on the Oakland waterfront. Earlier, London had been to the Last Chance only to discover that Heinhold had sold out, and without Johnny H. the place wasn't the same. So Jack moved on to the Hatch and almost immediately accepted Leach's challenge to have a go for a pitcher of beer. Leach had never been beaten. He had already won several pitchers that night from other challengers, but so far this bout was a standoff.

The barroom spectators cheered on challenger and champion as London and Leach each strained, gritted, and pumped every grain of his will and strength into the quivering muscle and fiber of his arm.

Almost imperceptibly at first, with the slightest movement, Jack began to force Leach's hand toward the table.

An inch, nearly two, and there it stayed, despite all the pressure Jack put forth.

At a table near a corner, two young, well-dressed men who were obviously out of their element watched the contest and sipped their beer as if it were champagne.

"Philip," the fairer and younger of the two men whispered, "let's get out of this place."

"Relax," Philip replied. "Enjoy your beverage."

Leach's arm dipped another inch and the cheering swelled.

The door to the Hatch opened, and out of the damp foggy night entered a big pea-coated sailor and a blonde. Her soft, corn-silk hair fell in unstudied waves past the curves of her shoulders. She was blue-eyed, with smooth lambent skin, full-lipped and full-hipped. Her attention went directly to the arm wrestlers and particularly to London.

Leach's face shuddered visibly now, and his arm shook. The spectators became suddenly subdued, sensing a finish. Then it happened; in a swift stroke, London slammed Leach's fist flat on the table, and there was an eruption of laughter, cheering, and clapping.

London shoved the empty pitcher toward the loser. "Fill 'er up, Leach," he grinned.

"No damn fair," Leach growled. "I was already spent from beatin' them other guys."

"Fill 'er up, Leach," London repeated.

Leach rose and grabbed the pitcher. As he did, he knocked against the table, wobbling it. London quickly put both hands on the typewriter to keep the rented machine from falling off. He looked at Leach, who was moving toward the bar, then Jack sat back and started to rub his wrist as the blonde flung herself onto his lap.

"Jack London! You son of a sea bull!"

She wrapped her arms around him and kissed him full on the lips. Jack responded fully. When they broke, London looked her up and down.

"Mai-mee! Everything's still in place!" He laughed. "Nothing's shifted."

"Yeah it has, London" came the big sailor's coarse voice. Scratch Nelson stood nearby, holding a sizable pocketknife—blade open—ostensibly cleaning his fingernails.

"Maimie's my dilly now."

London looked at Maimie, still on his lap, then to Scratch and the knife. His mind raced back to the Sunday morning five years ago when he had run to the wharf where the *Razzle Dazzle* was docked, to pay French Frank the agreed-upon price of three hundred dollars and take possession of the sloop.

French Frank had already moved out all his belongings— all except Maimie, the beautiful twenty-year-old girl who'd lived with him aboard the *Razzle Dazzle,* and who now looked with smoldering eyes at the sixteen-year-old boy casting gold pieces into Frank's hand.

"Three hundred," Jack counted.

"Three hundred," French Frank repeated. "Done and done. Here's the bill of sale. You are now the proud owner of the sweetest little boat on the bay." Frank was of medium build, swarthy-complexioned, with a pencil-thin mustache and a razor scar across his left eyebrow. He stuffed the coins into his pocket and threw a casual glance toward the beautiful girl sitting at the stern of the sloop.

London's look was not as casual.

She wore a soft summer blouse that barely contained the rich curve of her restless breasts. Her waist was compact but flared to ample hips and long, lovely legs that shot forth from beneath a pleated blue skirt. An unlit cigarette leaned out between luscious rose lips.

"Come on, Maimie," French Frank said. "Let's get going."

Maimie's eyes drifted from the ship's former owner and rested covetously on Jack.

"I'm staying," she said without looking away from London.

"You're what?" French Frank had heard her plainly enough but didn't believe it.

"I said I'm staying." Her look was still locked on the new owner.

"I've got all your stuff with mine," French Frank said.

"I won't need anything," Maimie replied.

"Like hell!" the Frenchman cried out. "You're coming with me." He started to board the *Razzle Dazzle* to retrieve his prize.

Jack London stepped between the sloop and her ex-captain. "Stay off my boat, Frank."

"What!"

"The *Razzle Dazzle* belongs to me." London held up the bill of sale. "And you're not welcome aboard."

"But *she* is! Is that it?"

"So long, Frank," said London. "Smooth sailing and safe harbors."

That night, under the splay of summer sky, the *Razzle Dazzle* dropped anchor in a small isolated cove, and the sixteen-year-old boy who had sailed and worked as a man entered manhood in another sense.

Never had Jack London been more aware of his own physicality, or of another's. Maimie torched his every sense, and fire shot through his every fiber. Her full, supple young body plied soft and warm in concert with his eager probings. She responded to his yearnings with almost savage harmony. Until the dawn they lay naked on the deck, lodged in each other's arms, alone in a private world that bobbed against the morning tide.

London removed his hand from Maimie's waist. Scratch Nelson pointed the knife toward his lady friend, who still sat in Jack's lap.

"I said, Maimie's my—"

"Sure, Scratch. Just saying hello to an old friend. I never staked any permanent claim."

Scratch folded the blade and motioned to Maimie. "Come on."

"Get us a drink, Scratch," Maimie smiled. "I'll be right over."

"Yeah, you will," Scratch answered, and moved toward the bar.

A sullen Leach Davits arrived, deposited a pitcher of beer on London's table and departed toward the front door.

Maimie leaned in and whispered. "Where'll I meet you, Jack?"

"Some other time, beauty." Jack smiled and pointed to the typewriter. "I've got work to do."

"You do remember the good old days . . ." Maimie purred, "and nights."

"I remember."

"They're still good."

"I've got work to do," London repeated.

"You've got to play sometime." She nuzzled at his ear. "I'll be around."

"Yeah." London saw Scratch watching from another table, and the look on the hulking sailor's face proclaimed that the wick of his patience was burning low.

London gently but resolutely boosted Maimie from his lap. "I'll see you around, beauty."

Maimie walked away, slowly swinging those hips, knowing that London still watched. His eyes went from the hips to the typewriter—and back to the hips. He tugged at his ear, audibly cleared his throat and his thoughts, poured beer from the pitcher into a glass, and swallowed the brew in one quaff.

As Jack poured more beer into the glass, First Mate Cyrus Spinner entered the Hatch, followed by Cookie. The two men walked past London to the bar, where Spinner threw down money and banged on the counter with his fist.

"Drinks for the house!" The mate proclaimed. "On Captain Diequest of the good ship *North Star*."

The proclamation was greeted with mixed reaction. The sailors welcomed the drink but were all aware of Diequest's well-deserved reputation.

"The *North Star*'ll be shoving off for a short haul in a few days," Spinner announced. "We're looking for a crew."

"You're looking for idiots," said London so everyone could hear.

"Everything from mess boys to AB's—now who'll be the first to sign on?"

"I'd sooner sign on at San Quentin," Jack said even louder.

"This don't concern you, London." Spinner looked from Cookie to the other sailors in the bar. "We're looking for men—not slackers who're afraid of an honest day's work." Spinner forced a laugh.

Jack London rose to his feet. Spinner's laughter faded. An ominous silence blanketed the saloon.

The younger, paler beer sipper sitting at the corner table tapped his companion on the shoulder. "Philip, if you stay, you're staying alone. I'm getting the hell out of here *now*."

"All right, Bobby, let's go," Philip replied, and the two of them edged quickly toward the door.

Three sailors at a nearby table downed their drinks, also rose, and followed the two youths.

Jack London walked—not fast, not slow—toward Spinner and Cookie at the bar. Only a few of the customers at the Hatch had witnessed Jack's dockside fight with Diequest, but within minutes, all of Oakland had heard about the brutal encounter. Those customers who had missed the earlier battle now thought they might have the benefit of viewing the young seaman in another bout. The anticipation built as Jack approached the bar.

London stopped within striking distance of Cyrus Spinner. Cookie stood just behind the mate's left shoulder.

"Am I afraid of an honest day's work, Spinner?" London asked.

"How's that?" Mate Spinner muttered.

"I asked you a question. Eight months I lived on that hell ship. Am I afraid of an honest day's work?" There was a storm signal in London's voice and stance.

Spinner stole a glance at Cookie, who looked as if he'd already had more of London than he wanted.

"I . . . guess . . . I guess," Spinner replied slowly, "that you pulled your share of the load."

"And I say the *North Star* is a hell ship." London looked square at Spinner. "Her captain is a thief and a murdering maniac—and her first officer's a pig."

London stood waiting. Cyrus Spinner first lowered his eyes, then his head.

It was over. There would be no blows, no blood, no battle. London turned and walked to his table. He lifted the pitcher of beer with both hands and drained it. He picked up the bundle and the typewriter and walked toward the door.

Misery, the one-legged, one-eyed sailor who sat in a chair near the edge of the bar, began squeezing music out of his accordion. One of the customers opened the front door for Jack and winked as he walked onto the foggy waterfront.

He was glad that Spinner had chosen to back down and that Cookie had had enough. Jack too had had enough: of fighting, of hitting and being hit. Of bruised ribs and face and knuckles. He wanted to quit fighting and even quit thinking about fighting. He would think of other things.

His mind immediately went to Maimie. He thought of their first night together, and of all the other nights and days aboard the *Razzle Dazzle*. Of lovemaking. But it wasn't actually love. He liked her well enough, and there was no question about the physical attraction on the part of both of them. Jack was still attracted. Besides the physical pleasure, there was an effervescence about her, a bright sensation of fun, and an excitement for life. But in no sense of the word was it love. Still, he wanted to be with her again, in spite of Scratch and his knife. Unfortunately, that would inevitably lead to another fight, so Jack tried to dismiss Maimie from his thoughts. Unsuccessfully.

He commenced to whistle a sea tune, "A Capital Ship," and turned a corner, walking through the dank, soggy night, still carrying the rented typewriter and the bundle containing his old clothes and three new shirts.

Jack ceased to whistle. He looked toward a side street where he heard the sounds and made out the silhouettes.

Three silhouettes, the sailors from the Hatch, were beating hell out of two other silhouettes, Philip and Bobby, the two overdressed young men whom they had followed out of the saloon.

London stiffened and overcame his initial impulse. He'd had his bellyful of fights. He decided to mind his own business. Go his own way. Out of harm's way. He started to walk away from the slaughter. He took two steps before he changed his mind. He set the typewriter and bundle down upon the cobblestoned street and charged into the fray.

The three thugs had already lifted Bobby's wallet and had turned their attention to Philip.

London grabbed one of the muggers and slugged him just as Philip went down in an unconscious heap. Bobby seized the opportunity to stagger against a garbage can, then disappeared down the misty street.

The other two bandits were digging for Philip's wallet as Jack charged into them. He did not do well. They turned upon him and gave him an expert going-over as the third assailant regained consciousness, dashed to Philip's inert form, pulled out his wallet, removed a handful of money, and threw the wallet to the ground.

The other two managed to knock London down, then ran off after the man with the money.

As they hotfooted it away, one of the muggers stepped directly on London's rented typewriter.

Jack staggered to his feet. For a man who had decided to eschew violence, he had taken a hell of a beating. He examined his new-used suit. It was ripped at the shoulder and lapel. He wobbled over toward the figure still sprawled on the wet street.

"Hey, mate," Jack said. "You hurt bad?"

No response from the mate.

London knelt over the unconscious youth. "Come on, lad, heave to. What's your name? Where do you live?"

Still no response. London picked up the wallet from the street to look for some identification. As he examined the wallet by the pale light of the streetlamp, a billy club bounced across Jack's head and he went down again, not quite out, but skin-close.

London managed to roll over and look up at the uniformed officer of the law with billy club raised to strike again.

"Hold up," said Jack.

"I'm holding," the officer replied.

"What the hell did you hit me for?" London rubbed the welt on his head.

"Why do you think?" The officer pointed the billy club toward Philip who was regaining consciousness. "I saw you trying to roll this dandy."

"Officer, you and I both made a mistake. Let me try to clear this up." London turned to Philip who now was sitting cross-legged on the wet street. "Hey, mate, will you explain to the Sheriff of Nottingham here that I'm on your side?"

Philip had pretty much come to his senses and realized what had happened. "Oh, that's all right, Officer. This gentleman came to my assistance."

"Yeah?" The officer was still suspicious and addressed London. "What's your name?"

"Don Quixote," London replied. Philip smiled at the riposte.

"What?" The officer asked.

"What's the difference?" London wiped at the blood on his face. "I'm bleeding to death."

Philip rose, winced at the ache in his head and ribs, and made his way toward Jack and the policeman.

"It's perfectly all right, Officer, I assure you. I'll take care of him. You can go about your rounds."

"Well, if you say so. I guess it's all right." The officer started to walk away.

"Thanks," Philip called out.

"Yeah, thanks," London added, touching the billy-club bruise. On his hands and knees, he crawled over to examine the damage to his typewriter.

Philip reached down and picked up his wallet, then walked to where Jack sat in the street.

"Many thanks," he extended his hand by way of introduction. "Philip Bambridge."

"Jack London," he said without looking up.

"Are you . . . all right, Mr. London?"

Jack thought a moment, then turned to face the inquirer while reviewing his condition.

"My new suit's torn. My rented typewriter's busted . . . and so is my head. Hell, fella, I'm sitting on top of the world."

◁ **CHAPTER 8** ▷

P HILIP UNLOCKED, THEN opened the door. Jack followed
him into the palatial entryway of the Bambridge home.
From some nearby room came the muted sound of a harpsichord.

London felt reluctant, unsure, particularly when he
walked. It was like walking for the first time on the deck of
a ship at sea. It seemed as if the floors were tilting upward,
then sinking with the roll of the ocean. He had never been
inside such a magnificent structure, with such elegant
furnishings and fine gold-framed paintings, all illuminated
by a crystal chandelier.

His immediate instinct was to turn and run away. Instead
he stood, swaying slightly, head swathed in Philip's blood-
soaked handkerchief, carrying the damaged typewriter in
both hands while Philip had hold of the bundle of old clothes
and new shirts.

Even though both men looked just like what they'd been
through, Philip's attitude was light, cheerful, and assured.
After all, this was his house, rather his mother's house.

"Well, come in, Jack. Come in!"

Instead, Jack took a step backward. "No, look, I uh . . . I
just thought of something."

"What?"

"I uh . . . I don't think this is such a good idea."

"Nonsense. The least we can do is take care of that crack on the head." Philip took Jack by the arm and led him toward the parlor and the music. "And do something about the suit and the typewriter."

As they entered the parlor, the girl at the harpsichord stopped playing and looked up.

Jack had been unaware that there was anyone anywhere in the world like this—a pale, ethereal creature of incredible delicacy, with wide, spiritual blue eyes and hair of spun gold, slender but shapely, and radiant, a girl who complemented such a setting.

She rose and came toward them. "Philip, what happened?"

"Nothing to worry about," Philip bantered. "Somewhat bloody, but unbowed! By the way, Jack, we mustn't bleed on Mother's carpet. Oh, Jack, may I present my sister. Felicity, this is Jack London."

Jack didn't know if he was supposed to shake hands, and since he still carried the typewriter, his confusion was further compounded. He managed to half nod, half bow.

"How do you do, Mr. London?" Her voice was light and lilting and perfect, thought Mr. London.

Felicity turned to Philip. "You still haven't told me what happened."

"Oh, that. We ran into a gang of muggers. Nothing Jack and I couldn't handle. They did manage to get away with my money, though." Philip pointed to London's head. "Could you see to that, Felicity? Ol' Jack can use some mending."

"Yes, of course," Felicity replied. "Mr. London, would you like to put down your typewriter?"

"Thank you, ma'am," Jack managed.

"I'll get the medical kit." Felicity smiled and started out of the room.

"Oh . . . and Felicity," Philip added, "hit the piggy bank for fifty dollars, would you?"

She nodded, cast an impulsive glance at London, and left.

Jack thought about setting the Oliver on a nearby table but quickly decided the delicate furnishing was too fragile for the heavy machine. Instead he put the typewriter on the carpet. Philip was on his way to the sideboard, where he poured a heavy dose of whiskey into two glasses.

"In the meanwhile," he observed, "we'll get a little medicine of our own. Take care of any internal injuries we might've sustained." He poured a dollop more into each glass.

Jack became more and more uncomfortable. The rich not only look different, he thought to himself; they act different and even smell different. The house had an aroma that Jack couldn't quite place. All he knew was that this manor had the scent of wealth—and he didn't.

"Cozy little mausoleum, isn't it?" Philip smiled on his way back from the sideboard. "Since father died, it's more than we can afford, but . . . here we are." He handed Jack the drink. "And here *we* are!"

Philip proposed a toast. "Confusion to the enemy! And Jack, thanks. Thank you very much."

Jack nodded. As they drank, Felicity entered holding a medical kit.

"Sit here, Mr. London." She indicated a chair.

"No, thanks," he stammered a feeble protest. "Look, ma'am, I'm . . . I'm all right. I've got to be going—"

"Sit down, Jack," she said kindly. "And will you please call me Felicity."

"Yes, ma'am." Jack swallowed the rest of the whiskey and sat, still holding the empty glass, while Philip made another journey to the sideboard.

Felicity removed the handkerchief from his forehead and efficiently went to work.

The touch of her fingers on his forehead sent a vibration

through the entire muscled mechanism of his body. It was a sensation he had never felt before, not even when making love to Maimie and the others.

Her palm was cool and soft as a rose petal but alive against the hard texture of his skin. He held his breath. He was afraid he would unmask his inner feelings if he spoke or even moved.

"It's quite nasty," she said, referring to the bruise as she softly touched his forehead. "Your head must be throbbing."

"Yeah . . . I mean no . . . it feels fine. I mean it feels better now."

Philip returned with a bottle and poured more whiskey into Jack's glass.

"This will hurt some," said Felicity as she dabbed iodine on the bruise. Jack was beginning to enjoy the pain.

"Yes, and I imagine those thieves are hurting some, too," Philip expounded. "Felicity, you should've seen ol' Jack here—sprang on them like a tiger—yes, that's it, a tiger! How does it go? 'Tiger, Tiger, burning bright, in the forest of the night' . . . ta, da, da, da, da. . . ." Philip had forgotten the rest. "How does it go, Felicity?"

" 'What immortal hand or eye," Felicity looked directly into Jack's eyes, " 'could frame thy fearful symmetry?' "

"Right!" said Philip. "Never could recall a line beyond that—I guess nobody can."

" 'In what distant deeps or skies,' " Jack found himself picking up the poem and returning Felicity's look, " 'burnt the fire of thine eyes? On what wings dare he aspire? What the hand dare seize the fire?' "

Both Felicity and Philip were amazed. Neither could have imagined those words remembered and spoken by this awkward two-fisted sailor. They tried unsuccessfully to conceal their amazement.

"You certainly know your Blake, ol' bucko." Philip took a shot of whiskey.

"He did create strong images," said Felicity as she continued working on Jack's bruise. "He was an extraordinary poet."

"And painter, engraver, composer, and philosopher—and most certainly a visionary," Jack added.

"What else do you know about him?" Felicity smiled.

"That he thought the world was mad," Jack said, and shrugged, "with bloodshed, cruelty, and selfish lovelessness, a world that turned little children into chimneysweeps and worse."

By now Felicity and Philip were absolutely awed by their paradoxical visitor.

"Is William Blake your favorite poet?" Felicity inquired.

"It's hard to pick a favorite," Jack answered "I think Poe had the most effective command of words and images among the Americans—and then there's Kipling, who has a lilt and swing and excitement about him."

"Yes." Philip finished off his drink. "And I'd say you have a bit of excitement about you, too, old bean."

"Philip!" The voice was imperial, and so was Mrs. Bambridge, who entered the parlor with mien and manner of royalty. A tall, still-slender woman of fifty years, with silver-blue eyes perfectly set in a classic face that was framed in perfectly coiffed silver-blue hair.

"Ah, Mother," Philip greeted her. "I thought you were asleep."

"Did you?" She looked down on London, then back to Philip.

"Mother, this is Jack London," Philip said. "We were in a fight."

"With each other?" Mrs. Bambridge inquired.

"No." Philip laughed. "Jack came to our rescue. Bobby Winters and I . . . I say, I wonder what happened to Bobby? You see, we were accosted—"

"In some bar?" Mrs. Bambridge arched a regal eyebrow.

"No, we'd already left the bar. It was out on the street. A

band of thugs jumped us—that's when Jack waded into them. You should have seen him finish them off."

"Yes, I'm sure." Mrs. Bambridge appraised London as Felicity continued her repairs. "What do you do, Mr. London, besides rescue wayward children?"

"Sailor," Jack said, clearing his throat. "I'm a sailor . . . and a writer . . . I think."

"What a curious combination. And what sort of writing do you do?" She glanced at the typewriter on her carpet.

"Oh, fiction. Articles. I'm going to start on a novel next . about the sea."

"Yes, well, I wish you good luck, thank you for whatever assistance you gave my son, and bid you good-bye." She turned and started to leave. "Good night, Philip, Felicity."

"Good night, Mother," brother and sister replied.

When Mrs. Bambridge left, they all breathed a little easier, especially Jack.

"She's not as haughty as she sounds." Philip poured another round."

"Oh yes, she is." Felicity smiled at Jack. "There . . . that ought to hold you together. You've been an excellent patient."

"Thank you." Jack stood up. "Well . . ." He drank his whiskey and was about to set his glass on a table when he thought better of it.

Felicity took the glass from his hand.

"Thank you," London said, and started toward his typewriter.

Without Jack's noticing, Felicity passed the fifty dollars, which Philip had forgotten about, into her brother's hand.

"What?" Philip exclaimed, then caught on. "Oh, Jack. Here." He held out the money.

Jack was obviously embarrassed. Felicity looked away, busying herself by fumbling with the medical kit while Jack mustered his pride.

"No, thanks," he said firmly.

"Oh, come on," Philip insisted. "It's just to cover some of the repairs. God knows I owe you."

"No," Jack repeated, holding the typewriter in both hands again.

"Yes!" Philip shoved the money into London's breast pocket. "And that's final."

Philip led the way, and the three moved toward the entry hall, Jack carrying the typewriter, Philip the bundle, and Felicity the medical kit.

As eager as Jack had been to leave the Bambridge house earlier, he was now sorry to be walking toward the door. The rough-hewn sailor had momentarily crossed the threshold of aristocracy, caught sight of another way of life. He had drunk from their exquisite crystal, sat on their fine furniture, and breathed a rarer air. And he had met Felicity Bambridge. Now he felt he was walking away from that moment, from Felicity forever. There was no way back into this world.

"Can you make it home?" Philip asked as they approached the door.

"Sure."

"Where do you live?"

"Over on Sixteenth . . . with my folks."

"Very good. Well, Jack, we'll see you again, have a couple snortolas together."

"Sure." Jack didn't believe it. He looked at Felicity for what might well be the last time. "Thanks."

"Good night," she said, and smiled.

Philip piled the bundle on the typewriter and reached for the doorknob. There was a knock from the other side.

Philip shrugged and opened the door. Standing there was a thoroughly disheveled and confused Bobby Winters.

"I say—Philip!" Winters exclaimed.

"Come on in, Bobby," Philip invited. "We were just wondering about you."

They all laughed. Except Bobby.

Jack entered without sound and closed the door silently behind him. He stepped from the tiny entry toward the dark parlor and heard an emotional voice that came from the darkness.

"Madeleine Duvier, dear Madeleine. We are all here—your friends on this side." The voice was plaintive, mysterious, but unmistakably Flora's. She was in a trancelike state.

Cramped around the small table with her were the silhouettes of John London, Eliza, an elderly couple, and the widower Duvier.

"It is us, Madeleine," Flora droned on. "Flora London, my husband John, and Eliza—Charlie and Mabel Krugheimer, your old neighbors, are here—and Maurice is here.

"All our love, all our strength together. We are calling to you in the dark beyond.

"Madeleine, we are trying very hard to communicate. Help us, Madeleine. We feel your presence. We know you are here. Give us a sign. . . ."

As Flora spoke, there were three soft raps in the darkness. The people around the table all stiffened, and then Mabel Krugheimer screamed at the sight.

Jack London had struck a match and held it just beneath his chin. The eerie, yellow glow distorted his bandaged head and bruised features into the face of a horrible basilisk.

◁ CHAPTER 9 ▷

A FEW MINUTES later, Jack sat in his room in front of the typewriter on his rolltop desk. He punched slowly at the typewriter keys—once, twice, three times—but the third key stuck on the paper. London reached into the carriage and freed the key. Again, slowly, his finger punched the keys five more times.

He rose from the chair and walked toward the mirror. The room was small and cluttered. The walls were completely hidden by makeshift shelves crammed with books. The furniture consisted of a chest of drawers, the mirror, a narrow bed, a bed stand, the rolltop desk, and a swivel chair.

Jack stood in front of the mirror, but he wasn't exactly looking at himself. He was looking at the bandage Felicity had applied. He touched the gauze that she had touched, glowed in the remembrance of the feel of her dovelike hands. His reverie was broken by three soft raps at the door.

"Come on in," he said.

Eliza entered.

"Oh, it's you." Jack smiled. "I thought maybe it was Madeleine Duvier."

"That was a pretty dangerous stunt, young fella," Eliza admonished. "Mother's still fuming."

"She'll get over it."

"Mm-mm," Eliza said, then pointed to the bandage. "And how did you get that?"

"Liza," Jack said, ignoring the question, "do you remember Maimie from the old oyster-pirating days?"

Eliza nodded. "She did that?"

"No! Well, I always thought Maimie was a beautiful girl . . . and I've seen a lot of girls all over the world—all kinds, all shapes, but—"

"But what are you leading to? How do we get to the bandage?"

"Tonight I met another girl. An angel, a heavenly angel."

"Oh, you had a few beers in heaven, is that it?"

"They don't serve beer in heaven. Whiskey. Expensive whiskey."

"And bandages?"

"I helped this fellow out of a jam—"

"A fight?"

"Right. He turned out to be rich, took me to his house, and his sister—"

"Turned out to be an angel from heaven with a bandage."

"That's it!"

"Well, mister"—Eliza looked around the room—"you're back on earth now."

"Liza, I'm gonna bust out of this place. And I'll take all of you with me—you and Mom and Dad."

"How, Jack?"

"With that, sweet sister." Jack pointed to the typewriter. "That's the golden chariot that'll carry us all out of the lower depths and into the sun." He walked toward the typewriter, then sat in the swivel chair and faced his sister.

"Don't be blinded by the sun, Jack. You know what happened to Icarus."

"I know what happens to the poor, miserable wretches in this life who work in the jute mills, the canneries, and ships like the *North Star*. They end up like Dad—numb and broken, helpless and hollow, bad off as Mammy Jenny was born. Not me. Not—"

"Not Jack London!" Eliza smiled. She walked to him, leaned down, and kissed him on the cheek. "You ride that chariot, Jack. Ride it for all you're worth!"

"Thanks, darlin'."

"But get *some* sleep." Eliza went to the door. "Good night. It's good to have you home."

After she left, Jack thought for a moment about the events of the evening. He turned the chair slowly and looked at the paper in the typewriter.

With one finger, Jack punched at the keys. Once, twice, the third key stuck again—and again he freed it. His finger hit the keys five more times.

He looked at the page. It was covered line after line with one word. Felicity.

◁ CHAPTER 10 ▷

THE BANDAGE, STILL stained with dried blood, was now taped onto the mirror as it had been for ten days. Stuck onto the wooden frame of the mirror were almost a dozen three-by-five cards. Each card had ten words written on it.

Jack was typing on the repaired Oliver as he had been for eighteen hours a day every day for the past two weeks. A row of hand-rolled unlit cigarettes lined an edge of the desk. Nearby was a bundle of handwritten pages. On the top page Jack had scrawled, "Diary of the Voyage of the *North Star.*"

He stopped typing, took the lit cigarette from his lips, balanced it on the edge of the desk, and read the last paragraph in the typewriter to himself. The bruises had healed, but Jack London looked terrible, hair unkempt, clothes wrinkled, dark shadows under weary eyes.

He typed an additional line, tore out the sheet, and placed it on a stack of finished work. There were eighty-five finished pages already there. He rubbed his fingers through his thick, twining hair and thought a moment of all the other pages he had typed since writing "Typhoon Off the Coast of Japan" and winning twenty-five dollars for the almost effortless literary endeavor.

After picking up the prize, Jack had thought he'd found his life's work and that it would be a lark. He would continue to write articles and stories, and the twenty-five-dollar compensations would flow like canal water.

Jack had written another episode about life at sea and sent it to the editor of *The Call*, who had sent it back without compensation. Writing was no lark. In the months that followed, Jack composed more than two dozen stories about sailors, hobos, miners, oyster pirates, and other assorted adventurers. He mailed the stories to every magazine and publication in the state and country—*Youth's Companion, Overland Monthly, The Black Cat, Atlantic Monthly, McClure's, Cosmopolitan*—all with the same result. Rejection.

Jack read all the articles and stories printed by these same publications, who paid two cents a word, twenty dollars a thousand. He found them light and frivolous, without life and color, with happy endings and lacking in sweat and real excitement. Still, those stories were bought and published. Jack London's were not. He would not and could not write in that style. His stories glorified those who fought for forelorn hopes; who struggled under strain and stress, tragedy and temptation; who coped with conflict and made life crackle with the force of their strength and passion.

He wasn't even sure his stories were read by real men. Maybe he was caught in the workings of some mad machinery; maybe he had poured himself into the stories and articles and mailed them to a machine.

He folded the pages properly, put them inside the long envelope along with the necessary stamps, sealed the envelope, pasted more stamps outside, and dropped the offerings into a mailbox.

The envelopes traveled cross-country and fell into a mechanical slot three thousand miles away, were processed by an unfeeling editorial machine, and were sent back untouched by human hands, along with a sterotypical form letter completely devoid of personalized comment. To Jack London, there was no living proof that any human had read and evaluated his work. It must be some fiendish, well-oiled, and organized machine. Rejection.

They all made the round trip between the Pacific and the Atlantic. Rejection.

As Jack gazed now at the eighty-five pages, a black thought passed across his mind. What if this, too, were rejected? The other stories he had written in days, some even hours. But this one would take weeks, even months, to finish. Never had he invested so much time and effort. His back and shoulders ached with it. His eyes were bleary, his fingers burst with blisters, his brain throbbed. What if all the work and the hurt added up to the same result? Rejection.

No. He wouldn't allow himself to think about that. He would think only of finishing what he had set out to do, and sometimes, as he glanced at the bandage taped to the mirror, he would allow himself the luxury of thinking about Felicity, briefly, then go back to work.

London took a clean sheet of paper and rolled it into the typewriter. He started to type, but paused and lit another cigarette, even though one still burned on the desk. He inhaled deeply, thought a moment, then typed. Soon the room was clouded by a weaving web of smoke. There was a knock on the door. London kept typing. Another knock.

"Come on in." Jack finally responded, and kept on typing.

Eliza entered carrying a tray of food. Jack's new-used suit coat was folded over her arm. She stood watching her brother bent over the typewriter.

"Jack."

No answer.

"*Jack*," she repeated.

"Uh-huh." He leafed through the diary, found what he wanted, then started typing again.

Eliza set the tray on the chest of drawers. There were books open and scattered atop the chest, the bed, and on the floor. The room was littered with dozens of crumpled pages that had been typed or partially typed, then discarded and flung to land where they might.

"Jack, this room smells horrible." Eliza moved a pace toward him, almost stepping on Melville's *Moby Dick*.

"Uh-huh."

"And so do you."

"Uh-huh."

Eliza spun the swivel chair around so Jack faced her.

Jack spun back toward the desk.

"Don't fool around." He resumed typing.

"Two weeks you've been riding that chariot. Are you listening?"

"Just let me finish this sentence, Liza. Liza, just let me . . ." he trailed off.

Eliza picked up the cigarette butt that was burning into the edge of the desk. There was a row of burns on the lip of the rolltop. She snuffed the cigarette into a butt-filled ashtray.

"It's a wonder we haven't all been incinerated. Jack, you're either going to die from nicotine poisoning, starvation, or self-immolation."

"What?" Jack finished typing the sentence. "What did you say?" He started typing another sentence.

She watched him for another moment. "Are you really interested?"

"In what?"

"In what I said."

"Liza . . ."

"I mended your coat." She tossed the jacket over his head, covering his view of the typewriter and everything else.

He turned to her, removed the coat from his head, and smiled. "Thanks."

"I don't know what for. At this rate, you'll be here the rest of your life. I know—we can bury you in the coat. And in the casket, instead of flowers, we'll plant old Oliver there," she said, pointing to the typewriter, "on your chest."

"What?" Jack was still fuzzy

"Of course, and we'll break up the rolltop and make the coffin out of that so you'll feel right at home. How does that sound?"

"Aw, come on Liza, what're you talking about dying for? Cut it out, will you?"

"Okay then, eat!" She motioned toward the tray.

"Yes." He nodded. "Eat."

"Jack, can you stand up and move around, or has your bottom taken root to that chair?"

"What do you mean?" He started to rise and stretch. "I'm in good shape. I . . . oh—oow . . ." His back was stiff, and his neck muscles bunched from stoop and strain.

"Jack. Eat, then take a walk or a ride on the wheel. Go throw stones in the ocean, breathe something besides this stale air. Get out of here for a couple of hours and let me clean up some of this mess."

Jack rose and made his way toward the tray of food. He took a couple of swallows from the glass of milk. "Milk." He grinned.

"Yes." Eliza nodded. "You *do* remember. And *that* is a sandwich. Now, Jack, be a good boy and eat the nice sandwich, and Liza will do a little cleaning up around here."

She began to pick up books from the floor.

"No!" Jack protested vehemently. "Don't! Don't touch anything. I know right where everything is. I know . . ." He snapped his fingers, dropped the sandwich back onto the tray, and flew toward the swivel chair. "I know what I wanted to say!" Jack London was typing again.

Eliza stood watching her brother. He was no longer in the small room of the frame house on Sixteenth Street in Oakland. From the intense look in those truant eyes, he might have been at the wheel of the *North Star*, hunting seals at Cape Jerimo, or locked in combat with some vicious enemy. He was somewhere else, living the words that leaped from the typewriter keys onto the page.

She knew it was no use trying to change him or his methods. He had to go on until the marathon was finished. He was young and strong and would endure until he put his story on paper.

Eliza smiled, then moved out of the room and shut the door behind her.

Jack didn't realize it, but more than an hour had gone by. As testimony to his progress, there was an additional page on the typewritten stack and two additional crumpled pages somewhere in the room.

He set fire to the cigarette slanting from his lips and rolled a fresh sheet into the Oliver. He started to type. There was a knock on the door.

"What the hell is this?" he muttered, then said louder, "Come on in."

The door opened, and Jack saw Eliza standing on the threshold.

"Liza, what the hell is this? You just left. What do you want now?"

"There's a gentleman here to see you," Eliza replied. "Mr. Bambridge."

"I don't know any . . . what?" Jack swiveled the chair around as Philip stepped into the room. "Philip! Come in! Thanks, Liza."

"Thank you, Miss London," Philip nodded.

"You're welcome, Mr. Bambridge, and do stay for a nice long visit. Jack needs some human companionship—he's been living mostly with dead authors for two weeks." She smiled and left.

"Well, Philip!" Jack rose and shook hands. "This is an unexpected breeze—uh, sit down."

"Where?" Philip looked around the cluttered room.

London shrugged. "Here, take my chair."

"Thanks, but here's a spot," said Philip, pointing to some books near a corner of the bed, "between Dana and . . . let's see . . . Milton. *Paradise Lost*. Well, I certainly hope that doesn't turn out to be prophetic. How's it going?"

"Good." Jack smiled. "The wind's at my back."

"More like a hurricane, I'd say. You wrote all this in two weeks?"

"Yes."

Philip picked up the title sheet from the typewritten stack.

"*The Wolf*. I thought it was a story about the sea."

"It is."

"A wolf at sea, hmm. Sounds interesting. I'd like to read it." Philip's voice became serious. "You know, if it's any good, I'll see that it's read by the right people."

" 'Right people'?"

"I thought of being a writer," Philip's tone became urbane again. "Everybody has. And while I have absolutely no literary talent, I *do* have literary connections, and I'd be pleased to use them in your behalf. But please remember, I said *if* it's any good." Philip winked.

Jack looked at the stringbean of a fellow sitting there and searched for Felicity in his face. There was a resemblance. The eyes were not as blue as his sister's, the hair was darker, and his features masculine, but the patrician Bambridge heritage shone through—the finely sculptured cheek and chin, the delicate arch of the nose, and the high forehead.

Philip replaced the title sheet, rose, and walked to the mirror. He spotted the bandage and looked at London, who avoided his glance. Bambridge pointed to the cards on the mirror frame.

"What are these?"

"Word lists." Jack moved closer. "I put up ten new words on a card every day and memorize them."

"How enterprising." Philip read the words from one of the cards. "Diehedral, dilator, dilettante—now that would apply to me—dilurial—well, so much for today's lesson. Let's move on to other topics."

"All right. What're you doing on this side of the tracks?"

"Oh, come on, Jack. Stop sounding as if you disapprove of the rich."

"I don't disapprove of them." Jack smiled. "I want to be one of them. Speaking of money, this belongs to you." Jack reached into his pants pocket and removed a roll of bills.

"What's that." Philip looked puzzled.

"Forty-nine dollars," said Jack.

"What are you talking about?"

"It cost exactly one dollar to repair the typewriter. This is your change."

"What about the suit?" Philip protested.

"Liza did the mending, so forget it!" Jack shoved the money into Philip's breast pocket. "And that's final!"

"Well, if I'd known you were going to do that, I wouldn't have come over to invite you."

"To invite me?"

"Yes, to a picnic."

"Where?"

"On the picnic ground, where else?"

"When?"

"Sunday. It's the Fourth of July."

"No." Jack looked at the typewriter. "Thanks, but I have to work."

"Nonsense. It's un-American to work on the Fourth of July. Besides, Felicity and I thought you might like to meet some of our friends."

"Felicity?" Jack hesitated. The opportunity Jack had thought would never come, and it might never come again. "Is your sister going to be there?"

"She is." Philip winked. "As a matter of fact, old boy, it was her idea to invite you."

"Who else?"

"Who else what?"

"Who else is going to be there? Your mother?"

"No." Philip laughed. "Just a couple of people our age from the university. And *you*."

"No." London was at a loss. "I'd better not—"

"Look here," Philip said with mock helplessness. "You're not going to make me go back to Felicity and tell her you turned her down?" Philip looked at the bandage stuck on the mirror, then from the memento back to London with broad theatrical supplication. "Jack, I know Felicity is not pretty; as a matter of fact, she's quite homely and over-weight, with a frightful complexion and completely devoid of personality, but Jack, you wouldn't do that to me . . . would you, Jack, old friend?"

Jack, of course, did not refuse the satirical importunings of his unexpected visitor. When Philip left, London was hard put not to leap up and down like some exalted gibbon at the zoo and swing by an imaginary tail at the prospect of seeing and perhaps touching the most exquisite and lovely creature in existence.

London looked at his reflection in the mirror and un-ashamedly made happy faces at himself. Sunday! Sunday! Sweet Sunday! Only four days away!

He stepped closer to the mirror and tore off the bandage, holding it in both hands. Sometime in the last two weeks she had thought exclusively of him. She had spoken to her brother of Jack London. She had said his name, had desired to see him and be with him, and had expressed that desire.

Ambition soared on sweeping eagle wings—there was nothing he couldn't do. He could conquer conquest. He would ride his chariot and write his book, and on Sunday he would see—and be with—Felicity. But suddenly he felt the need to lie on his book-laden bed; and rest and sleep, and recharge his mortal spirit, and hopefully dream of Felicity, and rise and write until he could be with her again on Sunday, sweet Sunday.

◁ CHAPTER 11 ▷

OAKLAND PARK WAS located along the estuary near the seaport. It was not so much a port of traffic as a port of rest and repair for the vessels with flags flying at the stern— flags of the United States and the other Americas, of Germany, Sweden, England, Japan, Norway, France, and Greece. The masts of the sailing vessels could be seen in the distance through the oak, locust, and eucalyptus trees of the park. And close by passed the slow schooners carrying hay from ranches in Sacramento and San Joaquin.

The park had an octagonal bandstand with pointed roof. Benches and tables were painted green, matching the thick summer grass.

That Fourth of July Sunday, the park was populated with picnickers of all ages and sizes, eating from their wicker baskets and blankets, sipping sodas and beer from bottles, pails, glasses, and mugs, setting off balloons and firecrackers, and playing a variety of games.

Jack London hovered above the ground in a horizontal position, his hands supporting the front half of his body, poised for the wheelbarrow contest. His legs were supported by Felicity Bambridge, who was having difficulty sustaining his weight.

Nearby, Philip Bambridge and Bobby Winters were in a

similar stance, supported by their partners for the wheel-barrow contest which was being overseen and directed by Philip, as was every aspect of the outing.

Philip's girl was Vivian Chapel, a slender brunette who spoke with a slight British accent, had violet eyes and a bright smile. She was a student at the University of California. Bobby Winters was propped up by Elsa Heinz, a sturdy, somewhat overweight blonde of German ancestry who was full of wienerschnitzel and gemutlichkeit. She looked as if she could have lifted Bobby above her head with one hand while eating cheese with the other.

"Wheelbarrow contest! Go!" Philip bellowed, and the three couples were off toward the finish line about twenty yards away.

The spirit of competition coursed fiercely in London and he was off to a good start, but Felicity couldn't hold up his legs. She dropped one, then the other, and Jack fell flat on his face, but still smiling.

Elsa, in her eagerness, quickened the pace and it was too much for poor Bobby Winters, who was built like a pipe-stem. His elbows buckled and he, too, went down.

Philip and Vivian sailed along at a moderate but steady pace.

Felicity lifted Jack's legs and they were off again, but only for a short distance. Again she dropped them and this time fell on London's back.

Elsa easily hoisted Bobby by his extremities and thrust him forward, but too late. Philip and Vivian effortlessly crossed the finish line first.

Philip assumed a standing position, winked, and patted Vivian's pink cheek. "Well executed, old girl. Exactly as planned."

Felicity lifted herself from London and smiled. "Sorry."

"My fault." Jack shrugged. "Too much ballast."

Close by, a half dozen children were flushing water out of a hand-pump and wallowing in the mudhole they'd created.

Philip produced three oranges from the basket on the bench and handed one each to Felicity, Vivian, and Elsa. "All right, everybody, gather 'round! Next is the orange transfer contest!" Philip gave brief details of the rules of the game, directed the contestants to their proper positions, then hollered, "Orange transfer contest! Go!"

Each girl had an orange tucked under her chin and clasped her arms behind her. The object was to run to their partners, who were waiting in a line twenty yards away, transfer the orange to the partner's chin without use of hands, and then the partner would run back to the finish line with the orange still wedged under his chin.

Elsa was off like a shot. She beat the other two girls by ten feet. But she thrust the orange at Bobby's neck with such ferocity as to damage his windpipe and cause him to drop the orange.

Felicity and Vivian arrived at about the same time. Vivian and Philip went about the transfer with practiced ease.

Felicity placed her chin and bosom against Jack, but he just stood there, staring and feeling the gentle weight of her body against his.

"Come on, Jack," she said. "Hurry!"

Jack snapped out of his reverie and the transfer was completed. He ran past Winters, who was squirming on the ground trying to clench the orange between his chin and breastbone while Elsa knelt beside him urging her partner on.

It was no contest. Philip and Vivian were again victorious. London looked back at Felicity, shrugged, and let the orange fall into his hand.

The youngsters by the pump continued to flush out water, make mudpies, and lubricate themselves with the black slop.

This time Philip produced three fresh eggs from the basket and reviewed the rules of the next contest.

"Egg-tossing contest! Go!" he exclaimed.

The girls and their partners were lined up about six feet apart. Each girl had an egg in her hand and, at Philip's signal, tossed it to her mate. All three catches were completed even though Jack had to move adroitly, yet delicately, to grab the fragile missile without breaking it.

The three men took two giant steps back and tossed. Miraculously, all three girls caught the eggs without breakage, but Felicity barely managed.

Jack smiled and formed a circle with his thumb and forefinger indicating 'well done.' Felicity responded with her charming smile.

Then the girls retreated two giant steps and prepared to toss. Elsa went first: the egg flew as if shot from a musket. Bobby flung his hand out palm up, the egg splattered yellow and white against it.

Vivian's egg arched perfectly and found Philip's waiting hand.

Felicity's egg looped high and wide in the air, but Jack ran straight under it and reached up with both hands when Maimie's voice blared out, "Ahoy, Jack London!"

Jack turned his face toward the salutation just as the egg smashed directly onto his forehead, then dripped into his left eye.

Scratch Nelson was at the reins in a wagon, with Maimie next to him and another couple in the backseat. They all exploded with merriment.

"Take a hinge at Jack," Scratch roared. "He's got egg on his face!"

Scratch drove the wagon off the road closer to London and the picnickers. Everybody except Felicity was laughing. She went to Jack and dabbed at his eye with a lace handkerchief, which was hardly adequate for the task.

"That's usin' your head, Jack." Scratch laughed again, drank beer from a pail, and passed it on to Maimie and the others. He turned his attention to Felicity. "Bull's-eye, ma'am! Give the little lady a cee-gar!"

Scratch brought the wagon to a halt just beside London and Felicity.

"I'm so sorry, Jack," Felicity said.

"It's all right." Jack managed a smile, put Felicity's handkerchief in his pocket, and wiped the remainder of egg off his face with his shirttail. "Hello, Maimie, Scratch. What're you doing?"

"Same as you," Scratch answered and took another mouthful of beer from the pail. "Picnickin'."

"Yes, well, hope you have a good time," Jack answered, and started to turn away.

"Jack," Maimie called out. "Aren't you gonna introduce us to your friends?" The friend Maimie was looking at was Felicity.

"Sure, this is Felicity and Philip Bambridge, Vivian Chapel, Bobby Winters, and Elsa . . ."

"Heinz," Elsa said heartily, taking Scratch's measure.

"I'm Scratch. This here's Maimie, and the two bringing up the rear are Ike and Sara."

"Well, so long," London said, hoping that would be construed as an amiable parting.

"Say," Maimie's elbow poked Scratch in the ribs, "this looks like a pretty good spot for our picnic, don't it?"

"Yeah, I'd say so," Scratch replied. "Let's drop anchor." He jumped off the wagon and lifted Maimie by the waist lightly onto the ground.

By now Philip had returned from the bench and was holding a rope. "All right, tug-of-war next," he announced. "Jack and I challenge Bobby and the ladies." Philip was determined to lose none of the contests.

Scratch winked at his companions. "Here, Jack. We'll challenge you good folks to a friendly tug o' war. How about it, ladies and gents?"

London sized up Scratch and his friend Ike, who was nearly the height and breadth of Nelson, then looked at the spindly Philip and even spindlier Bobby.

"No, thanks," Jack answered.

"Aww, come on," Scratch taunted. "You dandies ain't ascaird, are you? There aren't as many of us. How about it? Is it a go?"

"*No.*" London shook his head emphatically.

"*Yes,* it's a go!" Philip proclaimed. "We'll take them on, and I'll be anchor man."

Scratch and Ike grunted their approval and started rolling up their sleeves.

Maimie took a step toward Felicity and gave her the up-and-down. "Honored to meet you, I'm sure."

"Thank you," Felicity replied, also appraising Maimie and taking note of the way the beaming blonde kept looking at London.

Scratch and Ike drank more beer from the pail as Philip and Bobby stretched out the rope along the ground. Philip placed a handkerchief down at the center to serve as the boundary line, the proceeded to one end of the rope to act as anchor man.

"All right, team, let's get ready," he called out. "Jack, you take first position for our side."

Jack accordingly assumed the first post on his side of the rope, with Felicity behind him and the grinning Ike just opposite. Sara was behind Ike, then Maimie, and Scratch at anchor.

Scratch whacked Maimie on the rear and winked as she turned. "Hold on," he hollered. "I got an idea to make this a mite more interestin'."

London became even more apprehensive.

"Let's just move down this way a bit." Scratch, holding the rope, strolled toward the pump and the mud puddle. "Hey, you kids! Get outta there. Go 'way, beat it!"

The youngsters scampered away.

"The pump'll be the line." Scratch smiled at London.

"Oh, no, it won't!" Jack replied, looking at the pit of mud.

"Are you scared?" Nelson bellowed.

"No, we're not scared!" Philip decided.

"Just a minute." Philip quickly removed his shoes, then both socks, and rolled up his trousers. "Off with your shoes and socks, everybody—we'll give them a party."

Bobby, Vivian, Elsa, and Felicity also removed their shoes and socks. London seemed reluctant but finally took off his shoes, revealing a hole in his left sock. The sock came off fast.

Scratch's team stood barefoot and ready, as Nelson drained the last gulp of beer from the pail. "The contest's over when the anchor man's across the pump. All right! Ready?"

"Ready!" Philip called back.

London, of course, was nearest to the mud. "Yeah, ready," he muttered.

"Pull!" Scratch commanded.

The tug-of-war was on.

The rope stretched taut with Jack, Felicity, Bobby, Elsa, Vivian, and Philip on one side of the muddy pit and Ike, Sara, Maimie, and Scratch on the other. Things remained about even for a few moments, but then Scratch and company applied pressure, and Jack and company were drawn closer to the mud.

"No fair lettin' go, ladies and gents," Scratch reminded them. "You gotta keep a hold of the rope."

London's feet were being dragged perilously close to the mire, and so were Felicity's. Scratch let go of the rope with his left hand and gave Maimie another whack on her rump, then grinned, gripped the rope with both hands, and pulled harder.

Jack slipped in the mud and fell, as did Felicity. Both tried to get up, but a fierce snap of the rope from Scratch and Ike sent them sprawling again. Jack and Felicity were dragged through the slime past the pump, with Bobby, Elsa, and Vivian all dumped in the mud behind them, and Philip in imminent danger.

Just as it looked as if Scratch's team was going to win, Nelson eased up, and Jack pulled back. He and Felicity were forced to wade through the mud again, backward.

Scratch was having the time of his life. He reapplied pressure, propelling Jack, Felicity, Bobby, Elsa, and Vivian forward into the pit again. Back and forth it went twice more, with Scratch and his team high and dry and laughing—and Jack and his team getting muddier and muddier, as the still-unmuddied Philip continued urging his team to "pull, damn it, pull!"

The besplattered London had borne all he was going to bear. "Hold on, Felicity," he said, and spat out some mud. "Pull, Philip, pull!" Jack gritted his teeth, dug in both heels, and started a slow but inexorable pull back. His shoulders shuddered; his legs stiffened; his hands clasped like steel clamps around the rope. He pulled. One step back. Then two, three. Ike was in the mud. He fell and slid.

The blood pounded in Jack's temples, but back he pressed, and with him Felicity, Bobby, Elsa, Vivian—and of course Philip, the anchor man. Ike was face down in the mud on Jack's side of the pump. Sara was being dragged across the slush. With all his intensity and strength, London jerked hard on the rope, and Maimie and Scratch were propelled off balance, stumbled into the slimy ditch, and were hauled through the mire.

London's team, led by Philip, leaped up and down, proclaiming victory. Maimie and Scratch staggered to their feet, faces, clothes, and hands a muddy mess.

Jack London stood and watched as silence fell upon the proceedings. Scratch's fiery green eyes flared. He looked at London, then peeled away a patina of mud from his mouth, stepped forward, and extended a dirty palm.

Everybody laughed as the two muddy men shook hands.

"I say," smiled Philip, the only one still unmuddied, "that was fun, wasn't it?"

Simultaneously, Jack, Scratch, Ike, and even Bobby ran

toward Philip, picked him up, carried him to the pump, and threw him into the muddy ditch.

Hours later that night, Jack and Felicity sat leaning against an oak tree and watching the fireworks explode into the blue-black sky, cascading into variegated colors and showering down over the bay. Rockets and bombs streaked toward the stars, bursting and swirling and scattering into glowing ashes, landing on distant wine-dark water and cool, wet shore.

For the first time they had managed to be together, only the two of them. Without family, friends, or fools to interfere. His hard, callused hand held her soft, rose-petal palm.

For Jack there were no dipping ships at sea with lonely night watches on rain-drenched decks. No hiss of steam and wailing whistles on tilting freight cars with clacking iron wheels on curving rails of steel. No damp, dark hobo camps with simmering pots of watery rabbit stew. No smelly jails. No smoky saloons. No squealing seals. No blood and broken bones of forlorn seamen. No sailors lost at sea. There was only Felicity, her hand in his, on a warm summer night he wanted to last forever.

He sat there looking at the blazing sky, and saying nothing, almost afraid to speak, afraid of saying something wrong or coarse, or, even worse, of expressing what he felt.

For a long time he dared not even look at her, then finally he turned and saw that she was looking at him.

"I'm glad you came back," Felicity smiled.

"What?"

"I said I'm glad you came back from wherever you were. Where was it? Some South Pacific Island? Or at sea?"

"I . . . I'm sorry."

"Oh, it's perfectly all right. I only wish I could have been there with you."

"You were."

Her fingers moved slightly against the rough palm of his

hand. "Was I?" Then her voice changed as if she were reciting from a poem: "The night was dark . . . not a star or the moon could pierce the black masses of storm clouds that obscured the sky as they swept along before the gale . . . a soft light emanated from the ocean."

"Felicity," said Jack, "how did you know those lines? I—"

"You wrote them when you were seventeen and had just returned from the voyage on the *Sophie Southerland.* 'Typhoon Off the Coast of Japan,' published in the *San Francisco Call,* November 12, 1893."

Jack was still dumbfounded. "But you couldn't have remembered—that was years ago."

"No," she smiled, "it was just last week."

"What do you mean?"

"I mean I went down to the newspaper and looked it up in their files."

"Why?"

"Because I wanted to read something you had written."

"And you memorized it?"

"Oh, not all of it, but some parts. I can see why you won first prize. It . . . it's almost poetry—and William Blake isn't the only one who creates strong images. Jack London does quite well in that department."

"Thank you."

"Are you writing something like that now?"

"Well, not exactly, but it is about the sea. A novel."

"May I read it when you're finished?"

"Hell, yes! Oh—excuse me. I'm sorry, I . . . I'm really sorry. It's just that I didn't expect any of this to happen . . ."

"Neither did I, Jack."

◁ CHAPTER 12 ▷

IT HAD JUST become July fifth. Mrs. Bambridge sat alone reading in the parlor. The grandfather clock against the far wall struck for the twelfth time, then resumed its rhythmic ticking.

Florence Bambridge had been a widow for almost five years. She had been in her midforties when Miles Bambridge had died and left her with two children in their teens and enough money to live in reasonable comfort, but not nearly enough to live as well as she once had.

She thought of marrying again. She was a highly attractive woman, and not without passion. She had never given herself to any man before or since her husband's death. Their sexual relationship had been satisfactory—at least Miles had seemed satisfied. There were times when Florence wished he weren't satisfied quite so quickly and easily. But he was not a man of deep emotions or great strength. To him sex had its time and place and it was always at the same time and in the same place. After the first few months, Florence knew almost to the minute when and for how long she and Miles would be intimate.

In the last few years, half a dozen suitors had sought her out. The trouble was that those for whom she felt some physical attraction weren't wealthy enough. One, a younger man, was obviously seeking an early retirement from a failing business.

Those who were wealthy and willing to share their wealth and themselves were physically unacceptable. So for the time, Florence Bambridge would sleep alone and see to it that both her son and daughter married well and wealthy. Philip was bright enough, but hardly capable of earning a living, and Felicity could have her pick of the rich and eligible.

Florence Bambridge reached for the glass of warmed milk on the table next to her chair. She drank. The milk was no longer warm. She heard the sound of the front door opening, then the sound of laughter.

The happy threesome—Philip, Felicity, and Jack—had done their best to clean off the dried mud, but their clothes were still soiled and wrinkled. Philip carried the empty wicker basket in one hand and his seersucker jacket in the other. He set the basket on the floor and tossed the jacket onto a chair.

"What say to a little nightcap, Jack?"

"Well, it's getting pretty late—"

"Nonsense, the shank of the evening. Time for all good men to come to the aid of some brandy. Say, that Scratch seems like a pretty nice fellow, and Maimie—I've never seen any—"

"Good *morning*, Philip, Felicity." Mrs. Bambridge's clear cold voice interrupted as she swept into the entryway.

"Hell-o, Mother!" Philip responded.

Then there was silence. Mrs. Bambridge was reviewing the condition of the three young people.

"We've . . . uh"—Philip buttoned a button on his dirty shirt—"been celebrating the birth of our great country."

"In some pigsty?" Mrs. Bambridge cast a dissenting look at London.

"In the park," Philip answered. "You see, we met these friends who—"

"Philip, you're supposed to be a grown man. If you insist on frequenting waterfront bars, socializing with tramps, and wallowing in filth, that's one thing—but I would have thought you'd have more respect for your sister. Look at her! She looks as if she—"

"Mother, please!" Felicity was close to tears.

Mrs. Bambridge took a step toward her daughter. "I give you fair warning, Felicity. I don't like this . . . and I won't stand for it."

Mrs. Bambridge moved quickly past Felicity, brushed by Jack without acknowledgement, and strode up the stairway.

No one moved or spoke until the door slammed.

"I'm sorry," Jack said to both of them. "I didn't mean to cause any trouble."

"The trouble isn't with you, Jack. It's with Mother's obsolete middle-class sense of values." Philip extended his hand. "For which I apologize."

The two of them shook hands. Felicity came close and put out her hand. "Good night, Jack. I've never had such a nice time."

"Good-bye, Felicity."

London entered his bedroom. Although it was the depth of the night, the summer moon gleamed through the window, illuminating the room enough for Jack to see his reflection in the mirror.

He walked to the desk and picked up one of the cigarettes he had rolled, then sat on the bed and leaned against the brass headboard. He struck a match, lit the cigarette, and filled his lungs. The smoke felt harsh inside his body.

For a short, glorious time, he had allowed himself to be lulled out of reality. To be transported across the Slot, out of the slums of San Francisco, and into sublimity. To hold her hand and forget the stench of the world he toiled in. To erase the cruel unseen scars of the sea; of saloons, hobo camps, jails, and freight cars. Of jute mills and canneries. Like Marley's ghost he was bound by the links of a chain that had been forged since his birth.

For those sweet moments he'd shared with Felicity that Sunday night, he had allowed himself to believe that he bore no scars, no chain. That he, Jack London, could be the equal of any man, or woman.

But he had been slapped in the face with reality by a woman. Mrs. Bambridge.

He could still hear her voice slashing like a razor across his spirit: "If you insist on frequenting waterfront bars, socializing with tramps . . . wallowing in filth. . . ." That was Mrs. Bambridge's appraisal of Jack London. Tramp. Filth.

". . . I would have thought you'd have more respect for your sister. . . ." What would Mrs. Bambridge have thought and said if she had seen Jack and Felicity sitting together, holding hands and sharing dreams? What would the right and proper Mrs. Bambridge do if Jack London ever tried to see and be with her daughter again?

But why even think about it? It was over. Jack had work to do. He looked at the typewriter on the rolltop. Maybe he could write a couple of pages tonight.

No. He would start fresh tomorrow. He took off his clothes, folded them over the swivel chair, sat on the bed, and started to lie down. Then he remembered.

Jack London rose, removed something from his pocket, and lay in the bed. With the same hand in which he had held Felicity's palm, he now held her handkerchief—and slept.

◁ CHAPTER 13 ▷

THE NEXT MORNING Jack awoke still clutching the egg-stained handkerchief and still thinking of the sweet and bitter celebration of the day before.

He went to the bathroom, cleaned his face and brushed his teeth, and then attacked the typewriter.

An hour later Eliza brought him coffee and oatmeal. For dinner she brought him a sandwich, milk, some fruit, and removed the untouched oatmeal. For supper it was a bowl of stew, more milk, more fruit, and she removed the half-eaten sandwich.

Almost two weeks went by in this solitary confinement, and rarely did he leave the room. He read, and wrote in longhand. He typed. He reread, rewrote, and retyped.

The stack of clean pages dwindled. The stack of typed pages mounted. So did the discarded, crumpled pages that cluttered the room.

Twice Flora had insisted that Jack join the family for dinner. Both times he spent less than twenty minutes at the table, then headed back to the typewriter. Sometimes he would glance at the bandage still taped to the mirror, and for the few hours he slept each night he would hold the handkerchief. But he tried not to think of Felicity. He tried to think of nothing but the book.

Diequest. Spinner. The crew. The seals. The violence. Words. Sentences. Paragraphs. Pages. Chapters.

On the Sunday afternoon following the Fourth of July, Jack's father had knocked on the bedroom door and entered when Jack responded, "Come on in."

John London held his cane in one hand and in the other the unsmoked pipe that Jack had brought him as a gift.

Jack swiveled in his chair and looked into his father's flickering eyes. He scooped some books into a pile on the bed and made space to sit.

"Here, Dad, sit down. How're you doing?"

"I'm fine, son, but . . ." The old man sat on the cleared spot of the bed. "Well, just between the two of us . . ."

"What is it, Dad? What's the matter?"

"Well, Jack, I'm just a little concerned about you."

"Me? Why, hell, Dad, I'm in fine fettle. Growling and snarling like a tiger, strong as J. L. Sullivan and happy as a baboon."

"Oh, I don't know, Jack. It's just not natural. Closed up in the confines of this room . . . with no human companionship, not eating properly, not getting any exercise or taking a drink. It's just not natural. I'm, well . . . concerned."

"Now, Dad, don't you worry—"

"You said we'd spend some time together. Go fishing and sailing . . . and plant a little garden, grow the fattest, reddest tomatoes in Oakland. I'd like that, son. It'd be good for the both of us."

"I know that, Dad . . . and we will. But first"—he pointed to the desk—"I've got to finish this. I've just got to. I can't stop and start again. Do it in dribs and drabs. I've got to sail straight through. It won't take long. A few more weeks. Then it'll be you and me like Damon and Pythias. You'll be sick of the sight of me. Is that all right?"

"It's all right, Jack." The old man nodded weakly. "I understand." John London pulled a package of tobacco from the pocket of his sweater, along with a sheaf of cigarette papers. "I love the pipe you brought me, but . . . right now you'll have to do the smoking for the both of us— but not too much, mind you. And most of all . . . I love you, son."

In all the years he could remember, Jack London had never heard his mother speak those words.

"I love you, Dad."

When his father left, Jack went back to the typewriter.

The rest of Sunday, Monday, and Tuesday were a blur of words and memories of the *North Star*.

On Wednesday morning Jack was asleep, his head on his folded arms at the desk. The door opened, and Eliza came in with a tray of food. She placed the tray in its usual place on the chest of drawers.

Jack stirred. Eliza made more noise than usual, deliberately.

"Food, Jack—and mail." She took the letter from her apron pocket and put it on the tray, then left the room.

Jack ran his fingers through his hair, tried to clear his mind, and went directly to the envelope. His eyes focused on the name above the return address: *F. Bambridge*.

He quickly tore open the envelope and read the letter: *Philip and I will be bicycling in the park this Sunday at 2 pm. Felicity.*

◁ CHAPTER 14 ▷

JACK WAS UP before the summer sun dawned red across the hills. He had written late into the night and then risen even earlier to work and make up for the time that he would lose at his desk that afternoon. But how could he count the time as a loss when he would be with her?

He added the brief letter to his collection of mementos. He couldn't keep his mind from straying away from the typewriter. What would he say to her? What could he talk about? Had he exhausted his store of conversation? Would Philip stay with them, or would just the two of them be together again?

Would he touch her? Hold her hand again? He tried to keep himself from thinking other thoughts—more physical, more intimate. But he could not.

Jack straddled the bicycle and waited near the picnic area, off on a side path by a eucalyptus tree. He looked up and down the main road again as he had done a score of times within the last few moments. He pulled out his dollar pocket watch and checked the time again as he had done several times before. The hands showed 2:05. He shook the watch to make sure it was running and held it to his ear. Tick, tick, tick.

Back into the pocket went the watch, and he looked again to the left and right.

Felicity and Philip were twenty yards away, approaching on their bicycles. As they drew nearer, Jack rode out to rendezvous.

"Hell-o, Jack!" Philip greeted when they converged. He immediately semicircled his cycle and rode off in the opposite direction. "So-long, Jack!"

The two bicycles were tipped upon the ground. Jack and Felicity leaned against the same oak tree they had sat beneath the night of the fireworks. But now the afternoon sun was tilting westward toward the sparkling bay.

They hadn't spoken a dozen words in the half hour they had been together. When they sat, she had taken hold of his hand and held it tightly. She was still holding it—and even tighter, as if she were afraid to let go, as if his strength were being transfused into her.

He wanted to speak but had no notion of what to say. He tried to think of something light and funny. But nothing light and funny occurred to him. There must be something he could talk about. Then it came to him. There's always one thing. Simultaneously, they turned to each other and spoke.

"It sure is a beautiful—"

"Isn't it a gorgeous d—" She laughed. "You know, Jack, I do believe we were both going to talk about the weather."

"I guess you're right." He smiled.

"Isn't that stupid? I don't care a whit about the weather," she confessed.

"Neither do I."

"What have you been doing, Jack?"

"Writing. Just writing . . . and thinking about a certain oak tree and the Fourth of July and a girl . . ." His voice trailed off.

"That's funny. I've been thinking about a certain oak tree, too. What did you do last Sunday?"

"I wrote two thousand words." He grinned. "And you?"

"Oh, Philip and Mother and I spent the day at the Yacht Club."

"The Yacht Club." London nodded. "Of course that's where all we rich and eligible young men spend our Sundays."

"Of course," she teased. "You see, when a boy reaches twenty-one, he becomes a man. When a girl is twenty-one, if she isn't married, she's a spinster—at least according to Mother."

"Your mother's a wise old party." A touch of cynicism laced Jack's tone. "Did you pick out somebody who owns a big yacht?"

"You owned a boat once, didn't you Jack? The *Razzle Dazzle*."

"What do you know about the *Razzle Dazzle*?" Once again, Jack was surprised. "That wasn't in any newspaper."

"No, but Philip found out all about you. You were famous on the waterfront. They called you the Prince of the Oyster Pirates . . . and you had a princess."

"Felicity—"

"I could tell by the way Maimie looked at you—"

"Felicity, that was a long time ago."

"I know. It doesn't make any difference in the way I feel about you, but . . . ." She reached out and touched his face. "Would it shock you if I confessed that it does make me feel a little jealous?"

Both moved closer until their lips trembled and touched, gently at first. Jack had never known a kiss like this. He swam in a sensation of enchantment, then took her in his arms and pressed his lips and body against her and kissed her eyes and cheeks and throat and found her lips again.

"Jack," said Felicity, finally breaking away, "We've come a long way from talking about the weather."

"I guess we have." He smiled.

"I think we've come far enough. I'd better be getting back."

"Next Sunday, Felicity? Can I see you again next Sunday?"

She nodded.

◁ CHAPTER 15 ▷

JACK GOT HOME just before the rain started, and just in time for supper. He had stopped at the flower market and picked up two bouquets for Flora and Eliza.

Matilda Snod, Eliza's twelve-year-old piano pupil, was on her way out the door.

"Hopeless," Eliza whispered as Matilda walked into the light drizzle.

Jack bowed and presented a bouquet to his sister.

"Thank you, kind sir." She curtsied, then whispered, "Our beloved mother is in a foul mood—maybe these will help."

"Why do you go and waste good money on these stupid, smelly flowers?" was Flora's response upon receiving the bouquet from her son. "If you're going to buy something, buy something we can eat, not some damn silly flowers that'll be dead in a few hours. Supper's on the table. Eat."

They ate. At the table, John London said that he was glad Jack had gotten out of his room, even if it was just for the afternoon. Flora made no comment.

Within half an hour, Jack was back in his room working at the typewriter, while the rain spattered against the window.

For two days the rain persisted at the window while Jack persisted at the Oliver, taking only infrequent breaks to sleep, eat, go to the bathroom and occasionally glance at the mementos.

On Tuesday afternoon there was a knock on his door. "Come on in."

The door opened, and Elmer Dodson entered. He wore a dark cloak soaked by the rain. No hat. Wet, silvery coils of hair twisted onto his pale brow. Dodson coughed. At first he seemed drunk. But he was not.

"Mr. Dodson." Jack rose.

"Your mother said to come up."

"Here, take off that coat." Jack helped the old man remove his cloak. "Are you all right, sir?"

Dodson managed a meager smile. "Let's table that question and go on to more pertinent matters."

"Sit here, sir." Jack led him to the swivel chair.

"I thought I'd better come by, Jack," Dodson said slowly, "and read what you've done so far." He coughed again. "If you don't mind. . . ."

"No, of course not."

Dodson forced another smile. "There's nothing more useless than an old teacher in the summertime . . . or more lonely." He took a handkerchief from an inside pocket and wiped his face. "You know, my boy, when I was young, I used to love the rain. Walked in the wonder of it for hours, watched it replenish the earth, give life to everything that grew. When you're young, the rain is invigorating. But when you get to be my age, or at least in my condition, the rain is depressing. Because you know that soon you'll be planted in the earth and no amount of rain will make you bloom again . . . but I don't mean to wallow in melancholia."

"Can I get you some tea, Mr. Dodson?"

"No, no." Dodson took a pint bottle of whiskey from his pocket and placed it on the desk. "This will do." He repressed another cough. "Now then, where is the libretto?"

London set the typed pages in front of him. "I'm just a little more than half finished . . ."

"I wish I could say the same," Dodson remarked. "All right, you get out of here for a while."

"Yes, sir." London walked to the open door, then turned back to say something to Dodson, but the old man was already immersed in the manuscript.

Jack walked silently out the door.

In the kitchen, John London sat on a chair peeling potatoes, Flora was baking bread, and Mammy Jenny was pointing to the jars of preserves in the basket she had brought with her through the rain. "There's peaches," she indicated, "pears, cherries, and—"

When Jack saw his old nurse, he went over and hugged her. "Mammy Jenny, how come you're out on a day like this?"

"Just bringing by some preserves, Johnny. I know you got a sweet tooth. Here, now let me take a good look at you." She obviously did not approve of what she saw. "My, my, you look *terrible*. What happened to that flush in your cheeks . . . to that sunshine that was in your face?"

"He's buried himself in that room," Flora remarked from the stove.

"Jack's been working awful hard," said John London.

"Well, I don't like it one bit," Mammy Jenny affirmed. "You're all faded out. You've got to get out in the sun, Johnny. You hear me, baby?"

"I hear you, Mammy Jenny."

"Now you eat some of them preserves. They're good for you. And get out in the sunshine."

"What sunshine?" London laughed.

"I mean when it quits raining, and you know it." She patted the side of his face. "You need some color in those cheeks, and you've lost weight, too. I don't like it!" She picked up the basket of preserves. "Mrs. London, I'll put these away in the pantry."

"Thank you," said Flora.

The room fell silent as Mammy Jenny carried the basket

to the nearby pantry. John London reached for another potato. For a few moments there was only the soft sound of the paring knife scraping the skin from the potato, and of the rain pelting against the window. Finally, Flora looked up at her son.

"What's Mr. Dodson want?"

"He's reading what I've written so far. He's—"

"Jack," Flora spat out emphatically. "Even if you do finish that book, even if it does sell—and that's a mountain of an if—it'll be a long time before we see any money. Isn't that right?"

Jack nodded.

"We need money *now!*"

"But I gave you almost three hundred—"

"That was a long time ago. We owed nearly that much from last winter—the grocer, the rent, doctors for your father, medicine. Bills! Bills! Bills! You want me to show them to you? Don't you believe your own mother?"

"I believe you, Mom."

"Then face the facts of life. You're the man of the house. We can't live off the few dollars Liza makes from giving those piano lessons."

Mammy Jenny was through placing the preserves but stayed in the pantry away from the family discussion.

"Flora"—there was desperation in John London's voice. "Maybe I could get work as a watchman somewhere—"

"Somewhere? *Where?* Who'd hire you? You're a sick man, too sick to work. No." She turned back to her son. "Jack, you've got to get a job and that's all there is to it!"

"But my book—it'll just take another—"

"*Damn* your book! What about us? Don't you recognize your obligation to us? After all the years we—"

"All right, Mom!" Jack slammed his hand on the table. "All right! You'll have your money!" He turned and walked toward the kitchen door.

"Where do you think you're going?" Flora called out.

"I'm going to walk in the rain and watch the wonder of it . . . while I'm still young."

Jack London walked through the warm summer rain. He didn't know how far or for how long. It didn't matter. All that mattered was that he had survived for almost twenty-one years. Survived deprivation—a mother who had never been a mother, a childhood without having been a child. He had survived the savage streets while hawking newspapers, the sordid saloons while swamping fetid floors, the bowling alleys, the freight trains, the Fish Patrol, the jute mills, and the hell ships—the fists of men who tried to maim and even kill him, the surging sea that sought to smash the ships and drown him.

He had known the hollowness of hunger; despair that he had tried to drown in whiskey. He had suffered the splintered hopes of success in rejection after rejection from editors of every publication where he had submitted stories.

All that was on one side, the dark side, as he walked the rain-soaked streets of Oakland and contemplated the prism of his life. But there was another, brighter side to that prism. Jack London was far better off than most of those with whom he had worked, sailed, tramped, drank, and fought— far better off than those who had been drowned, stabbed, shot, beaten and maimed, much better off than those who were wearing prison stripes in Folsom and San Quentin.

Jack London was young and strong, with an alert mind and an agile body. Despite the weeks he had spent pent up in his room with short rations of rest and food, his mind and body still coursed with fire and passion.

Passion. There was Felicity Bambridge, a new lustrous ray of the prism. On that first night at the Bambridge home, he had never dared think that he would see her again, take her into his arms and kiss those soft, sweet lips. But it had happened and it would happen again, next Sunday. And beyond that? What would become of them? How long could they be together? How long before she failed to resist some rich, eligible suitor from the Yacht Club? He didn't know, but as of now he knew she cared for him. Somehow he would succeed, not just for her, but for himself, for Jack London.

Succeed. He had succeeded in writing down one hundred and ninety pages of a novel that could be his passport to success. A novel that Mr. Dodson was reading at this moment. Mr. Dodson! A horrible stab of doubt punctured London's rain-soaked reverie. What if his old teacher didn't like what Jack had written? What if Mr. Dodson thought it was terrible?

Jack London ran back toward his house.

He stood near the doorway inside his bedroom and watched as Dodson, unaware of Jack's presence, read the last page of the unfinished manuscript.

Jack remembered the words that he had written, the words Dodson now read. It was the chapter about Smitty, sick with scurvy, denied by Diequest the slight hope of recovery—too weak to work and lacking the will to live.

Dodson put down the last page, and only then realized that his former pupil had returned. For long moments he looked at London, whose rain-drenched shirt clung to his body.

The old man rose and slowly put his cloak around his shoulders. Still silent, he walked to the doorway. His fevered eyes locked into Jack's. The old man's lips trembled, but still he said nothing.

Then Elmer Dodson embraced the young man. He clasped his arms around Jack London with all the strength that was left in him. When Dodson drew back, there were tears in his eyes.

He smiled and nodded and left without speaking.

London stood for a long time, then walked over to the desk and looked at the pint of whiskey.

Elmer Dodson hadn't taken so much as a sip.

◁ CHAPTER 16 ▷

NAKED, FELICITY BAMBRIDGE stepped from the frost-white tub and reached for a towel.

Instead she caught the reflection of her smooth, gleaming wet body in the mirror. Seldom had she paused to look at herself. But now she turned away from the thick pink towels stacked on the wallrack and examined her naked profile reflected on the doorway's full-length mirror.

She was tall, almost five feet seven inches, and undressed appeared less slender and more curvaceous than when garbed in girdling apparel.

She wondered as she stood looking at herself, why her thoughts went to him. She had known Jack London less than a month, but found herself thinking of him often, too often, sometimes in the parlor where they first met, while she played the harpsichord. She had thought of him when she rode her bicycle and could feel the muscles in her thighs and calves tensing and relaxing. She thought of him when she lay in bed with her summer-light nightclothes and waited for sleep. And she thought of him now, this strange young sailor who yearned to be a writer, this man-child.

He was uneducated in the formal sense—socially inept and awkward. Still he had memorized Blake and was conversant with Poe and Kipling. He probably had read ten, twenty or a hundred times more books than she had read, and not because they were assigned by some indifferent teacher at the university but because he *wanted* to. Because he craved to read and learn.

He probably had never been to the opera or a museum but he had consumed the library. He had never worn evening clothes but had sailed to Yokahama and trod on distant islands where naked natives danced beneath a crescent moon while the Southern Cross gleamed low across the sky.

This man-child of many contrasts, whose lips trembled at the touch of hers but who had lived openly with the sensuous Maimie.

Maimie. Felicity looked again into the mirror and could almost see the image of the ripe and carefree girl whose flashing eyes and careless golden curls bounced on her shoulders as she walked with swinging strides and smiled her sizzling smile. She had been Jack London's girl, his mate. And Felicity could tell by the glint in Maimie's eyes that she would relish the opportunity to be his girl again, and his mate.

Felicity had seen statues at the museum, some with fig leaves and some without, and sometimes the girls she knew would giggle and twitter and talk too graphically, but Felicity had always walked away from such tasteless conversation.

On several occasions she had started to ask her mother questions that occurred to her and every girl her age, but as soon as Florence Bambridge realized what was coming she changed the conversation to a more suitable topic.

And now Felicity gazed at her moist and naked body and felt the countless tiny tingling sensations that raced across her flesh.

◁ CHAPTER 17 ▷

JACK LONDON HELD the small black hand of the seven- or eight-year-old boy and walked into Mammy Jenny's backyard.

As usual, the yard was filled with lines of clothing hung up to dry. Mammy Jenny was taking freshly washed clothes out of a big basket and pinning them on a line.

"Here he is, Mrs. Prentiss, I brought him over, just like you said."

"You surely did, George, just like I said." Mammy Jenny reached into the pocket of her checkered apron. "And here's two pennies for you, just like I said. One for going and one for coming back."

"I thank you," George said, eagerly accepting his wages. "I thank you, Mrs. Prentiss."

"You are welcome, Mr. Wilson." She grinned and watched as George Wilson ran off, then she turned back to London. "You know, Johnny, with all this rain we've been having, I haven't been able to get much washing done. Look how it's all piled up and people wanting back their—"

"Mammy Jenny," Jack interrupted, "what's the matter? What's wrong?"

"You know what's the matter, Johnny." She became

serious. "And I thought you knew where to come if you needed anything."

"I don't need anything, Mammy Jenny, honest."

"Did you forget that I was there when your mother talked to you yesterday? When you walked out in the rain looking for pneumonia? And you standing there telling me you don't need anything. You need money, Johnny, and you're going to get it. I got over four hundred dollars saved and . . ."

"No!"

"What do you mean 'no'?"

"I mean I'm not going to take any money from you."

"Johnny, aren't you like my own son? Didn't you drink of my milk? Didn't I loan you money for the *Razzle Dazzle*? Weren't we partners in the oyster-pirating business? Weren't we?"

"We were."

"And didn't you pay me back with plenty more?"

"I guess I did."

"No guessing about it." She pulled out a roll of bills from another pocket of the apron. "Here's three hundred right now, and you're welcome to the hundred that's left if you need it."

"No!"

"Why not?"

"That was different."

"How different?"

"I knew you'd get that money back. I was buying something tangible, a boat. And there was big profit in pirating. But I don't have anything tangible now. I'm writing a book. It's just paper. How do I know it's going to sell? No, Mammy Jenny, I can't get further in debt. This time I got to pay my way as I go along."

She put her hand gently on his shoulder. "How're you going to do that, honey?"

"By doing like Mom says. Getting a job. I'll find one.

There's not much that I can't do. I'll find one that nobody else'll take if I have to. I'll get a job."

"I s'pose you will. But working all day, when are you going to write that book?"

"At night."

"When're you going to sleep?"

"When I finish the book." Jack smiled. "That ought to satisfy Mom."

"Johnny, you go easy on your mother. She's gone through a lot—a lot more'n you know." She patted the side of his face with her large warm hand.

"You know, Mammy Jenny, sometimes I get the feeling that there is a lot I don't know about myself and them." He looked at her eyes. "Is there something I ought to know that you can tell me?"

"Johnny, if there was—don't you think I would?"

London nodded. "I know you would. I'd better be going, let you get back to work and see if I can find some." He smiled and started toward the picket gate.

"If you change your mind, here I am." She grinned and held up the money. "And here *it* is!"

London smiled, waved, and walked away.

When he was gone, so was the grin on Jenny Prentiss's face. She still kept the dark secret she had harbored for over twenty years.

From six in the morning until nine at night, on Thursday, Friday, and Saturday, Jack had systematically covered the waterfront, markets, jute mills, canneries, saloons, laundries, theaters, restaurants, newspapers, and every place that might offer the prospect of employment. All with the same result. Negative.

As he came out the rear door of the Nighthawk Saloon into the alley, a would-be thief was making off with his bicycle. Jack ran after the culprit, tackled him and the bicycle, knocked the man almost senseless against a garbage can, and began to examine the damage to his wheel.

The man staggered to his feet, wiped the blood from his nose, and asked Jack's forgiveness, saying he was desperate and hungry, not having eaten for two days. Jack forgave the inept felon and gave him five cents for soup and bread.

Jack's original hope was to find a job as night clerk in some hotel, even one that catered to the ladies of the night, where he could pass out keys and write his pages in longhand so as not to disturb the comings and goings of the guests.

But the hope of finding such employment was dashed at every desk where he applied. After the hotels, he had gone down the line to the mills, markets, saloons, restaurants, laundries, then to any place at random where he might make a dollar a day to take home to Flora and family.

The sad and simple fact was that there was no employment opportunity—in sad and simple language, no job—to be had on the mainland. He had run into former shipmates who were going to sail again, and who urged Jack to join them, but so far Jack had declined. He didn't want to leave his home and family and ailing father so soon again—and he didn't want to leave Felicity.

On Sunday afternoon he waited on his bicycle at the park. This time Felicity and Philip arrived four minutes early, and once again the gallant Philip promptly peddled away in the opposite direction.

A few minutes later, Jack and Felicity sat beneath the oak tree. He kissed her tenderly and held her hand too tightly.

She sensed that there was something wrong. That he was somehow different than he'd been the week before. She put her fingers to his face, then softly stroked the errant hair that had twisted onto his forehead.

"Jack, are you all right?"

"I'm fine, Felicity—just a little tired, I guess."

"How's the book coming?"

"Progress. Mr. Dodson came by—he was my teacher at Oakland—and read it."

"Did he like it?"

Jack nodded.

"But, I should be further along." He smiled. "Except lately I haven't been able to concentrate like I used to. Keep thinking about a certain oak tree—and Sunday afternoons."

"So do I." She kissed him lightly. "Jack I've got some bad news."

London's face clouded.

"What is it, Felicity? You're not going to tell me that we can't meet anymore, are you?"

"No, not that bad. It's only for a month. Mother's been invited to stay in the country with friends, and she insists that I go along. I tried to get out of it, but there was no dissuading her."

"A month . . ."

"You'll be busy with your book—chances are, you won't even miss me," she teased.

"I'll miss you all right. But I'll be busy with something besides the book."

"What do you mean, Jack?"

"I mean I've got to find a job and fast."

"Well, that shouldn't be difficult for a man of your many talents."

"You've never had to look for a job," he flared. "Neither has Philip, or any of the Bambridges. I—" For the first time he had hurt her. He had momentarily forgotten how unused to reality she was. He was tired and angry, and he had struck out at her. Felicity's lips quivered. She had never heard or imagined that tone in his voice. Her face turned away from his.

"I'm sorry," he said, and touched her chin and turned it toward him. "I'm truly sorry, Felicity. I shouldn't have spoken like that. It's just that I've been trying everywhere on the mainland, and I don't want to ship out again . . ."

"Oh, Jack, that would mean you'd be away for months, wouldn't it?"

"Don't worry, I'll find something. I've heard they're going to be hiring at the power plant tomorrow, and guess who's going to be the first one belly-up in line?"

"The power plant? What kind of work . . ."

"I don't know, Felicity, and I don't care. Whatever it is, it'll be better than killing seals a thousand miles away from you. Won't it?"

She nodded, and they embraced.

"I'd give you the address of where we're going to be, but we can't take a chance on Mother, so if you have any news, send it through Philip—he's staying in town. One month! One long, dreadful month . . . but I can write to you—and I will. . . . I'll try not to be too passionate in my prose—I'll write about the weather and the cows and chickens. Oh Jack, will you miss—" But her lips were covered by his, and his arms held her tighter than ever before.

◁ CHAPTER 18 ▷

JACK LONDON, ALONG with more than a dozen other men of all ages and sizes, stood with his collar turned up against the morning cold, moving his feet in the damp dawn, waiting at the employment entrance of the Oakland Street Railroad Power Plant. Every few minutes another job seeker joined the herd.

Jack had been the first to arrive, followed by three others who introduced themselves as Scotty, Red, and Shannon. As more men came, nobody bothered with introductions, and the mood grew silent and sullen. The more applicants there were, the less chance each had of getting a job.

"Damn," said Scotty. "This is the coldest, wettest summer I ever knew."

"It'll warm up after a while," Red remarked without looking up from the newspaper he was reading.

"What time is it?" Shannon asked.

"About five-thirty," said London.

"What time did you get here?" Scotty inquired of Jack.

"Four-thirty."

"You musta skipped breakfast," said Scotty.

"Hell," said Shannon, shoving both hands into his jacket pocket. "I ain't et since yesterday noon. How many they puttin' on?"

"Don't know." Scotty shrugged.

"What's coal passin' pay?" Shannon asked.

"What does anything pay?" said Scotty. "Ten cents an hour."

"Well, what do you expect?" Red folded his newspaper and pointed it at Scotty. "With wheat at forty-nine cents a bushel and six-cent cotton?"

As Red spoke, a man bigger than all the others, wearing a black turtleneck sweater and black cap, shouldered his way to the front without saying a word and ended up next to London. The big man lit a cigarette, striking the match on the rear of his canvas pants.

"And with jobs scarcer than hen's teeth," said Scotty, casting an unfriendly look toward the big man. "Where's it gonna end?"

"Revolution," said Red. "That's where it's gonna end."

"This is still the greatest country in the world," Shannon affirmed as his stomach growled.

"Who says it isn't?" Red confirmed.

A smallish man with pince-nez spectacles and hawklike authority cut his way through the crowd.

"All right, let me through," he commanded, adjusting the beige derby he wore.

"Why?" Scotty asked.

"Because I'm Peter Pierce and I do the hirin' around here, and you need not apply."

"I didn't mean anything, brother," Scotty apologized.

"It doesn't matter anyhow, *brother*," Pierce clucked. "You're too small. We need muscle around here. Now who was first in line?"

"Me." The big man exhaled cigarette smoke and took a step toward Pierce.

"No, you weren't," said Jack, and moved in front of the big man.

The man turned to London. "Sonny, are you labeling me a liar?"

"No," Jack replied. "You are."

"Get outa the way, sonny, or you'll get stomped."

"Not today." Jack stood his ground.

"Today. . . . and now." The big man reached out to shove London.

Jack kicked him in the shank. The big man bent. Jack's left pumped into the man's belly, the right crashed into his jaw. The man bounced against the brick wall and sank to the sidewalk.

Pierce looked at the man lying in the street, then at London. "What's your name?"

"London. Jack London."

"Well, London, that makes you first in line."

"What about the rest of us?" someone shouted.

"Yeah, how many jobs you got?"

"One job," said Pierce, "and it's filled. Good day, gentlemen, we've got to get to work."

A few minutes later, Jack and Mr. Pierce were walking into a grimy, cavernous cellar room.

"London, I like your spunk. Times are hard, rock-hard, but if you work like you fight, you can make good here. There's opportunity."

"Just show me the job, Mr. Pierce."

"Here's where you start . . . at the bottom. But a good man can work his way to the top."

Pierce stopped in front of a mountain of coal. There were two shovels stuck into the pile, and on either side half a dozen wheelbarrows. A whistle blew. Pierce took out the pocket watch from his vest, adjusted his pince-nez, and checked the timepiece for accuracy.

"Six o'clock, straight up," Pierce affirmed and pocketed the watch. "Yes, sir, a good man can work his way to the top. Like Horatio Alger."

London looked at the slag of coal, then back at Pierce, and nodded.

A dozen men—wheelers—filed into the room and moved

toward the wheelbarrows. Pierce pulled out one of the shovels and handed it to Jack.

"All right, London, starting now, you're a coal passer. Keep them 'barrows movin'." Pierce took the other shovel and walked away. London removed his coat, hung it on a hook in the brick wall, rolled up his sleeves, and started shoveling coal into the nearest wheelbarrow.

The wheelers began to cluster around him. Jack nodded a greeting, but their attitude was less than friendly.

"You the man?" one worker asked.

"I'm the man," said Jack, and kept shoveling.

Jack London thought that he had known the racking ache of work before, but nothing he had done on sea and land—above, below, and on the decks of ships; at laundries, canneries, and jute mills—none of it spelled *work* as did the job he toiled at now for ten cents an hour, ten hours a day.

His wrists were swollen, his back stiffened, his legs were twin columns of agony, and his arms and shoulders throbbed, but still he shoveled. London shoveled coal into an endless sluice of wheelbarrows ten hours a day, six days a week, breathing the black dust from shovel and slag. Ten backbreaking hours each day with half an hour for dinner at noon, eating in five minutes and sleeping for twenty-five. Writing at night, fighting to stay awake, to put one page after another, one sentence after another, one word after another.

And then Sunday, blessed Sunday—when he could sleep for twelve hours and write for the other twelve. Monday, it was back to the shovel, the black coal, and the wheelers who seldom spoke a word to him. Six more days of gasping toil, six nights straining to stay awake at the typewriter, collapsing and waking with a start at the sound of the alarm clock.

The only relief from the insane routine were the letters

from Felicity. He read and reread them, smudged them with the grime of coal that would not wash from his fingers, pressed them to his lips, and kept them with his growing collection of mementos.

At three o'clock in the afternoon of the second Sunday, as Jack worked at the typewriter, there was a knock on his door.

"Come on in," he responded and turned to find Philip Bambridge.

"Your sister said I could knock only if I heard the typewriter, otherwise you'd be asleep, and that you've been killing yourself."

"Philip! What're you doing here? Has anything . . . is Felicity all right?"

"Far as I know, she's perfectly fine," Philip said with a smile, "but you'd know better than I. The only time she writes, it's all about you and how much she's missing you, and would I pop by to see if you're all right—so here I am. Now let me take a look. I say, old boy, you *have* gone to seed. Lost weight, circles under the eyes, sallow and sooted complexion. What the hell has happened?"

"*Work*, Philip, *work*. One word that isn't in your vocabulary—or experience."

"You're right about that, old fellow, but let's not be nasty about it."

"Of course, Philip, and I apologize. I shouldn't have said that. It's not your fault that you have money and don't have to work—and that I don't . . . and do."

"I think I follow that, and even agree." Philip nodded.

"It's white of you to occasionally mingle with the slum folk, to—"

"Oh, come on now, Jack. That's not fair!"

"No? I suppose you and your friend weren't slumming that night at the Hatch? I suppose you hadn't crossed the track for a little amusement with the hoi polloi. And I suppose you weren't amused by the ragamuffin who came to your rescue—"

"Jack! Maybe you're right about some things. I don't profess to be an egalitarian and don't deny being a diletante, maybe being guilty of having no discernible purpose in this universe, but one thing I *do* admit being guilty of is having a genuine respect and admiration of your mind, your talent and tenacity, of your ability and potential . . . at least until this visit, else why would I have encouraged and arranged for you to be with my sister whom I love?"

The room fell silent as the two looked at each other. Jack took a step forward and breathed deeply.

"Philip," he almost whispered, "I wish I had that shovel I work with, here in this room now. Do you know why?"

Philip shook his head.

"I'd give it to you and plead with you to beat my brains out if you could find them."

"And I'd be happy to oblige," said Philip, reverting to his usual tone.

"I've been working too long, sleeping too little, and getting madder and madder at the world. I apologize, my friend—you just walked in at the wrong time."

"Yes, my entrances have been somewhat ill-timed lately. Dismiss the matter from your mind, old boy. It never happened. Now, at the risk of being castigated again, let me ask—this work you're doing at the Inferno or wherever it is you labor, how much money do you earn?"

"Ten cents an hour, ten hours a day, six days a week."

"That does amount to six dollars a week, does it not?"

"It does."

"And"—Philip pointed to the typewriter—"all the time you're trying to finish your novel?"

"I am."

"Jack, at the risk of further incurring your irrational wrath, how would you react to the suggestion that I advance you a couple hundred? Just a loan, mind you, an advance!"

Jack London began to laugh. It was not the usual sort of light laughter that lasts half a minute or less. This was a deep, gut-wrenching laugh that came from every aching inch of London's weary body. He hadn't laughed like this in months, on the ship, before or since, or ever.

Philip watched, puzzled, waiting for the laughter to ebb. But Jack continued. He sat on the edge of the bed and laughed for a full two minutes more. Finally, Philip approached and put a patronizing hand on Jack's shoulder. "I say, Jack. Are you all right? Would you mind telling me what is so hilarious?"

"No, Philip." Jack finally controlled himself. "No, I wouldn't mind. But I don't know if you can appreciate the humor of it."

"I'll try."

"Here I am working myself toward insanity . . . maybe I already am insane . . . for ten cents an hour, when twice, *twice* I've been offered the loan of the money I need . . . and here comes the really funny part: once from a former slave, and now from a scion of society. How is that for extremes?" London laughed again.

"You'll have to excuse me for not joining you, old bean. You were right—the humor of it does escape me. Speaking of joining, I have one last suggestion. I am going slumming tonight. Would you care to join me for supper at the Yacht Club?"

Jack rose and gave Philip a hearty smile and a heartier whack on the arm.

"No, I wouldn't, but thank you, Philip. Thank you from the depths of my heart."

"For the invitation?"

"No. For coming here. For the laughs. For being a friend . . . and most of all, for putting things in perspective."

"I say, I did all that?"

"Yes, you did."

"Well then, I've done enough." He smiled. "And Jack, you've given me some perspective, too. I think Felicity is a very fortunate girl. I'll be cheering for both of you."

◁ CHAPTER 19 ▷

THE OAKLAND STREET Railroad Power Plant paid its employees every two weeks. On the second Saturday, Jack London received the twelve dollars he had earned as coal passer. He had also earned the approval of Peter Pierce. The hawklike little man lifted his derby, scratched at the half-dollar bald spot on the top of his head, and remarked, "You're making good here, London. Keep up the good work."

London folded the twelve dollars, went home, unfolded the bills, put eleven dollars on the kitchen table while his mother stirred the stew on the stove, then went to his typewriter. Not a word was exchanged between mother and son.

Both Eliza and John London attempted to talk Jack into writing less and sleeping more, but he waved them away and went on typing.

Sunday had been notable due to Philip's visit, but Monday it was back to shovel and load. On Tuesday, as two wheelers, Cleery and Tomkins, approached with empty barrows, Tomkins looked at Cleery and nodded. The decision had been made.

"Hey, London," Cleery said, and tapped Jack, who kept

shoveling. "I'm gonna tell you something we wasn't gonna, but hell, it just ain't human."

"What?"

"Pierce is playing you for a sap. That's what."

"I knew what I was doing when I hired on." London kept shoveling.

"No, you didn't," said Tomkins. "Pierce fired two coal passers before he put you on."

"What do you mean?" London stopped shoveling.

"Don't you understand?" Cleery shook his head. "For ten cents an hour, you been doin' the work of two men."

"Well," Tomkins grunted. "What're you gonna do about it?"

London looked at the two men and at the other wheelers who had gathered, then at the tower of coal.

"I'm going to keep them barrows moving." He started shoveling again.

For two more weeks London shoveled and thought only of two things: the pages he would write that night, those thousand words that he had made his nightly quota before allowing himself the indulgence of sleep, and of that Sunday when Felicity would be back and they would sit beneath the oak tree in each other's arms, when he would touch her instead of the letters she sent.

For two more weeks, that thought kept him going; each word he wrote and each shovel-load of coal brought him closer to that Sunday and Felicity.

◁ CHAPTER 20 ▷

Jᴀᴄᴋ Lᴏɴᴅᴏɴ ᴡᴀs asleep. Not on his bed or at his type-writer, but as he leaned against the oak tree while Felicity sat next to him, holding his callused hand and looking at his pale, haggard face.

Philip had tried to prepare her by commenting that Jack had been working too hard, that he had lost weight and color. Still, she was shocked at his worn appearance as he straddled his bicycle and waited for her along the road.

He had brightened at the sight of her, and some of the luster returned to his tired eyes as he held and kissed her hungrily, told her how beautiful she was and how much he had missed her. If only he knew how much she had looked forward to and welcomed those words and caresses, how desperately lonely she had been without him. Tenderly, she touched his face, his throat, and held his hand almost like a little child until he had fallen asleep. But it was no child's hand she held.

Gently, she let her thumb trace across the lacerated knuckles ingrained with grime that soap and water would not wash out. Only time would erase the coal dust that had coursed its way into the creases of his battered hand—and only if he quit the power plant.

Suddenly London wrenched his hand away and vaulted

into consciousness, not quite knowing where he was or with whom, until he saw the face that he had been waiting for a month to see. He rubbed his eyes and looked at her apologetically. "I . . . I'm sorry, Felicity. Guess I fell asleep."

Once again she took his bruised and swollen hands in hers. His fingers were trembling. "Jack, you're killing yourself."

"I'm all right."

"Is it that important?"

"What?"

"The book."

"Nothing's more important," he shot back fast, too fast. He realized how it sounded. "I didn't mean it . . . not like that."

"I understand," she whispered.

"No, you don't."

"All right, then." Her voice grew stronger. "I don't. I don't understand this insane frenzy. I don't understand what you're trying to prove by it. I don't understand it at all!"

"Just that I'm a writer."

"But, Jack, that'll take time—"

"I've already spent time."

"Years. Some men—"

"Some men—but not me! I'll find out now."

"Jack . . ."

He rose, not worn and haggard but his strong and vibrant self again, knowing exactly where he was and what he was saying and doing.

"Listen! Listen to me, Felicity. There's a line from one of Shakespeare's plays—it goes something like this: 'There's a tide in the affairs of men which taken at the flood leads on to fortune—omitted all the voyage of their lives is bound' "—Felicity joined him in finishing the line—" 'in shallows and in miseries.' "

"Yes, Jack," she said. "I know the line."

"And I know this summer is my tide. I can feel it, Felicity.

And that book is flooding up inside me. If I can put it down on paper, that could be my fortune—if I fail in that, well, then maybe it's shallows and miseries. But I'm not going to fail. That's why it's important."

"All right, Jack." She nodded.

"To both of us." He moved close and lifted her to him. He kissed her and held her with the encircling strength of his arms and pressed her to him until their bodies melded. "I never thought I'd find anyone like you. Until this summer, I never knew there was anyone like you. Felicity, I don't want to lose you. Just stay with me, Felicity. Don't go away from me."

"Oh Jack." She put both her hands on his face and kissed him. "Where would I go? Don't you know I love you?"

As he rode his bicycle home, he passed saloon after saloon and kept on wheeling. He thought about the times a few years ago when he would have stopped at every one—sometimes with Maimie at his elbow or on his knee, and other times when it was "men only" even though more than half the men were too young even to vote—and hardly anyone bothered.

They were all too busy raiding and drinking and fighting off the Fish Patrol—Jack London and his pirate companions, Scratch Nelson, Joe Goose, Nicky the Greek, Whiskey Bob, Soup Kennedy, Spider Healy and the rest. Risking prison stripes and pellets from scatter-guns as they raided the beds and cashed in with forty, fifty, sometimes over a hundred dollars apiece for a night's work.

And what did London and his companions do with those profits for which night after night they risked their lives? Did anyone bank a single dollar? Make payment toward a house or lot on which to build a house? Invest in stocks or bonds? Or buy a business? A saloon? A shop? No. Each did the same thing with his money.

Squandered it—on booze, gambling, women. Sometimes

the order was scrambled, but always the results were the same. The next day would find them all with hangovers and empty pockets. Jack was only sixteen years old, but he kept up with every one of them and often led the way.

Jack London had been on both sides of the chase. First as an oyster pirate raiding for profit and fleeing from the Fish Patrol, and then, when he saw too many of his mates dead on the deck, or bleeding, drowned, or behind iron bars, he accepted an offer from Sheriff Charley LeGrant.

LeGrant admired London's sailing ability and kindled a warm feeling for the likable lad. The sheriff suggested Jack put on the badge of the Fish Patrol and become a deputy. There was no salary, but there was adventure, and a half share of the fines levied against the lawbreakers they pursued and captured.

Jack thought the badge would induce him to change his ways. To stop drinking and carousing and to put a little money aside. Besides, the *Razzle Dazzle* had been sunk.

So Jack joined the Fish Patrol, and got his badge and share of adventure and booty, but soon found out that the deputies were just as whiskey-wild and reckless with their money as the pirates. After nearly being killed by Chinese shrimpers and finding himself broke and floating in a drunken haze somewhere off Mare Island Light, where the swift ebbs of the Vallejo and Carquinez Straits struggled with each other and almost dragged him under, he decided he'd had enough of pirating and patrolling, of whiskey, wanton women, and the rich rewards and young corpses that went with it all.

He bade farewell to Maimie on one of the most memorable nights either one had spent up to that time or since, then set sail on the *Sophie Southerland* for the Sea of Japan.

But he thought now, as he neared his house and typewriter, of all the money he had let slip through his fingers— hundreds, thousands of dollars—and how tomorrow he would return at six in the morning to the Oakland Street

Railroad Power Plant and shovel coal into the perpetual parade of wheelbarrows, to be fed into the hungry furnaces, where its energy was transformed into steam and electricity, while with each shovelful, the energy drained from London's body.

Once again he took solace in the fact that he was better off than most of those whom he had sailed with, around the bay and in the deep waters of the Pacific. After all, he was Jack London—and best of all, Felicity was home again.

Three more days and nights, Jack kept to his routine with cracked and blistered fingers—the shovel by day, the typewriter at night, with three and sometimes four hours sleep to recharge the muscles of his body and the battery of his brain.

On Thursday night the routine was rudely broken. The knock on his door came from a hospital orderly. Jack had been urgently sent for, and now a weary London was being led into the ward room by the night nurse.

"He can't last much longer, Mr. London," the nurse whispered. "He keeps calling your name."

Jack nodded. They approached the last bed, where another nurse kept vigil over the semiconscious Elmer Dodson. The first nurse left as Jack stopped at the side of the bed and looked down at his old teacher. His features were almost skeletal, and his breaths were protests against the final intruder. But the smell of death was all around.

"Mr. Dodson, it's Jack. Jack London."

"Jack . . ." Dodson's eyes opened, and his cold lips creased into a smile. "I knew you'd come. I . . . waited."

"I'm here, Mr. Dodson."

"Jack . . . the book . . . is it finished?"

"Almost, sir, just the last chapter."

"The . . . last chapter." Dodson nodded, coughed, and caught his breath. "You know I'm dying, Jack."

"No, you're not."

"I am, but it's all right. Jack, you're the son I never had . . ."

London tried to fight the tears, but it was useless.

The old man gasped for air and then went on. "On the table, my pocket watch—take it, put it in your hands . . ."

"Mr. Dodson—"

"Do it, Jack.

London looked at the nurse, then reached and took the watch and heavy gold chain and held it in his palm.

"Gold-filled, Jack . . . I want you to have it as a remembrance—and Jack, I want you to use your time better than I used mine . . . promise me . . . and I hope I helped you some. That seems to be my only legacy. Give me your hand, Jack . . ."

London took hold of Dodson's hand.

"Thank you, Jack, that helps. . . . My century's dying, too . . . and yours will soon be born. You wanted my suggestions . . . I don't have a damn one, I . . ."—he breathed a tranquil breath—". . . just didn't want to die alone."

Jack London knelt at the side of the bed and held the old man's hand with both his own, until life let go of Elmer Dodson.

◁ CHAPTER 21 ▷

ON SUNDAY AFTERNOON Jack met Felicity again. He showed her the watch and told her about Elmer Dodson's death and the subsequent events. Lawyer L. L. Llwellyn had come to Jack's house on Saturday evening carrying a black briefcase in one hand and a white urn in the other.

Llwellyn explained to Jack that he was a friend of Elmer Dodson's as well as counselor and executor of his estate. The lawyer was not a man to squander time. In accordance with Dodson's will, Llwellyn immediately had the remains cremated and was now delivering same to London, along with all of Dodson's cash assets, minus certain expenses, such as hospital and crematorium costs and, of course, Llwellyn's legal fee. It was all duly documented: Total cash in account (Bank of Oakland), $303.80—minus hospital expenses $54.70, crematorium charges (including use of urn) $25.00, legal fee $150.00.

Lawyer Llwellyn brought the balance in cash—$74.10— and deposited it into Jack London's hand, and in the other hand Llwellyn deposited the urn containing Dodson's ashes, along with the deceased's request that London scatter the ashes in the bay so they would float with the tide out to sea—the sea that Dodson had read about but never sailed.

On Sunday morning Jack gave Flora fifty dollars, rented a

small boat, carried out Dodson's last request, returned the urn to the crematorium, then bicycled to the park to meet Felicity.

"As I watched the ashes float away, I kept hearing his voice, Felicity—'I want you to use your time better than I used mine.'"

Jack looked at the watch and chain in his hand. "A gold-filled watch and three hundred dollars, the sum of a man's life. A good man. A learned man. An unselfish man. I *will* use my time, Felicity. I'm going to cram every minute of life with living, and I'm going to make it mean something."

Just after noon on Tuesday, at the Oakland Street Railroad Power Plant, Jack London was sitting on the floor near the base of the coal pile and leaning against the brick wall.

He had just finished a sandwich. He was about to peel an orange, but threw it back into the paper bag and decided to get a few minutes sleep. He dropped his head onto his arms, which were folded across his knees, and immediately dozed. But not for long.

Someone tapped him on the shoulder. London looked up at the workman gathered around him. Their dirty faces were grim. Cleery held out a cap. It had some money in it— a few dollar bills and a lot of change.

"What's the matter?" London asked.

"We're taking up a collection." Cleery moved the cap a little closer to Jack's face.

"What for?"

"For Jim Dawson's widow and three kids."

"Who's Jim Dawson?"

"He's one of the two men whose job you took."

"What happened to him?"

"He couldn't find another job," said Cleery. "So he blew his brains out."

The men stared at London.

"Anything you could see fit to contribute," Tomkins added, "would be appreciated."

Jack pulled the wallet out of his back pocket. He had folded a ten-dollar bill in one corner in case of emergency. He lifted the bill from the wallet and placed it in Cleery's cap.

Peter Pierce sat at the rolltop desk in his small office eating his noon meal when the door burst open. Pierce wheeled around and saw London step into the room.

"What the hell do you want?" Pierce exclaimed.

London held a shovel filled with coal dust in his hands. Jack flung the contents of the shovel onto the startled Pierce, covering his face, body, derby, and desk with sooty black grime.

"I quit!" London dropped the shovel and left.

Cleery, Tomkins, and all the other workers cheered Jack London as he walked away forever from the Oakland Street Railroad Power Plant.

"Felicity, I am asking"—Florence Bambridge's eyes narrowed with dire implication—"no, I am demanding that you come to your senses! This whole thing has gotten out of hand, and it must stop immediately, do you hear? Immediately!"

"Mother, nothing has gotten out of hand. We haven't—"

"Never mind what you *haven't*; I know what you *have*. You have been making a spectacle of yourself with this brute. You wrote him letter after letter while we were away, and you've been sneaking off to see him every Sunday afternoon at the park and God knows when and where else."

"Did Philip—"

"No, Philip didn't. But I'm nobody's fool, Felicity. I had you followed."

"Followed?"

"I gave you fair warning, but you have persisted in pursuing him like some bitch in heat!"

"Mother!" Felicity covered her face with both hands.

"Never mind playing Miss Modesty with me, young lady—the time has come for plain talk and hard facts. Felicity, one foolish hour with this . . . this sailor, and your life can be ruined—all the sweet moments of your childhood, all the plans of your father's and mine, all our hopes, dreams, and ambitions for you, ruined. Don't you think he'd take advantage of you as sailors do, as I'm sure *he* has done with women of every country and color? They only care about one thing—making a conquest or concubine of every woman they meet. Or has he talked to you of love and marriage?"

Felicity said nothing.

"Well, heaven help us, has he?"

"Not exactly . . ."

"*Not exactly?* Well what exactly can you expect to come of this? Look at him and then look at yourself. You are a lady, Felicity, used to the fine things in life, and deservedly so. You were born and reared as a lady should be—with charm, beauty, manners, and grace. And look at him—an ape . . . an ape from the sea."

"He is not an ape."

"He is crude, brutal, coarse—poor, uneducated, and without prospect."

"Mother, I'm not clever with words like you, but you don't know him. He's not the things you say. He would never take advantage of me, never—I know it. Yes, he has sailed and fought and drank and been with women—"

"Probably has some disease!"

"That's a contemptible thing to say, Mother!"

"It is a contemptible world he lives in, not your world at all. It never can be."

"Everyone can't be born rich and refined. He's had to work ever since he was a child, and it's true he never graduated, but he has a brilliant mind. He's educated himself, read more books than all the Bambridges put together with the Crockers and the Stanfords thrown in. He's not a brute; he is a sensitive, considerate human being, and not without prospect. Jack will be successful."

"At what?"

"At whatever he puts his mind to. Even now he's writing a book—"

"Some penny dreadful, no doubt. Have you read it?"

"No, but neither have you. Why must you condemn him?"

"Has he ever been published? Has he ever earned one red cent from his literary endeavors?"

"Mother, he's not even twenty-one years old—"

"And neither are you. What do you know of worldly matters? Besides, I don't give a damn if he is Byron, Shelley, and Keats combined—he is still not for you!"

"And who is? Some fop from the Yacht Club? Some frilly fool like—"

"Philip? Like your brother Philip? Is that what you were going to say?"

"No, it isn't. I love Philip, but—"

"You wouldn't want to marry someone like him, is that it?"

"Mother, what's the use? You won't let me finish a sentence. You keep putting words in my mouth."

"I'm trying to put some sense in your brain." Mrs. Bambridge's tone softened, and so did the look in her eyes. "Oh Felicity, I love you. You and Philip are all I have. I want to see you both happy, warm, and protected always. There are a hundred young men who would leap at the opportunity of giving you all in life you'd ever need; handsome, healthy, and wealthy young men, men of your own class and culture. At first you might think there is something romantic and adventurous about this London, but pause for just a minute and picture yourself with him years from now, living in some garret, boiling soup while he's trying to sell some stupid story, or worse, left alone with child or children while he's off for months or years on some ship halfway around the world."

"It wouldn't be like that—"

"Felicity." Florence Bambridge moved to the parlor window where her daughter stood and placed both her hands gently on her shoulders. "I'm going to tell you something I thought I'd never tell a soul. But this is too important. I *do* know something of how you feel . . . you see, I once had my Jack London, someone too much like him, only he wasn't a sailor.

"It was shortly after the war. I was just about your age. I suppose he was what they called a cowboy. He had brought the first herd of cattle to St. Louis all the way from Texas. He was tall and strong and wild, foreman of the outfit, and he, too, aspired to wealth and position. He was going to have a ranch of his own, the biggest in Texas, and more money than any boss he'd ever worked for. He was no ordinary cowboy, not Blake Morton. We met in the dining room of the most elegant hotel in St. Louis—I know because my father owned it. Blake Morton sent the most expensive champagne to our table, charmed the entire family, and swept me off my feet and almost into his bed.

"I thought I loved him, even though I knew him for only a few days. He wanted me to marry him and go to Texas. I barely resisted the temptation, thanks to a conversation like this one with my mother and father. But something about him frightened me. He was too strong and wild and dangerous.

"Blake Morton wrote me every week and was going to send for me when he bought his ranch. I never went to Texas—three months later Blake Morton was dead, killed in a bar in Abeline. Strangely, I didn't feel a thing, except maybe relief.

"So now you know about my wild and reckless love. Later

I met and married your father, a warm and gentle man, and shared a blissful life and cried my eyes out when he died."

"Mother, I never dreamed—"

"No, of course you didn't."

"But times have changed, and Jack London is not Blake Morton. If only you would get to know him better. We're not going to do anything rash and foolish, I promise. Meet him again. Talk to him, give him a chance. That's all I ask. Please."

"All right, Felicity, if that's the only way you'll have it. I will meet and talk to him. Tell him to come by Sunday."

"You mean that, Mother? Do you?"

"Of course I do. Sunday, say at six."

◁ CHAPTER 22 ▷

Less than an hour after London walked away from the Oakland Street Railroad Power Plant, he walked into the Hatch. He hadn't even stopped to wash the coal dust from his face and hands.

The Hatch was doing good business. The tables were nearly filled with sailors and their women, drinking, some playing cards, some singing to the accompaniment of Misery, the one-eyed, one-legged sailor who squeezed out a tune on his accordion.

Maimie and Scratch sat at a corner table. Nelson waved for London to join them, and Jack acknowledged with a nod as he proceeded toward the bar and free-lunch counter.

"Well, hello, Jack," Baldy, one of the bartenders, greeted him. "Ain't seen you in a spell—what'll you have?"

"Jingle up a whiskey and a beer to start, Baldy. I just might get pipped today." London reached for a sandwich and put money on the bar.

Baldy served up a whiskey and beer but shook his head. "Your money's no good, Jack."

"Why not?"

"Captain Diequest's buying." Baldy pointed to a table where Diequest, Spinner, and Cookie sat.

"It's Diequest's money that's no good." London shoved

the coin across the counter closer to the bartender. "Ring it up."

London walked over to Misery, who had a tin cup pinned at the knee of his limbless pantleg, and dropped in a coin. The sailor nodded, smiled, and kept squeezing out music.

Jack went back to the bar, downed the whiskey, and walked, beer in hand, toward Maimie and Scratch. To get there, he had to walk past the captain's table.

"Mr. London." Diequest sipped his whiskey and smiled. "How've you been?"

"Much better, since stepping off the *North Star*."

"Well, I'm happy to hear that, but we're shipping out for Japan again. Thought you might like to sign on. Ten-dollar bonus, twenty a month and found. You made a handsome profit on your last voyage, remember?"

"I remember." London took a swallow of beer. "And I heard you were having a hard time gathering a crew."

"You heard wrong," Diequest replied easily, and looked London up and down. "How's the writing going? By the sight of you, it must be pretty grimy work."

Spinner, of course, did not miss the opportunity to laugh at his master's remark.

"Did you ever finish that book?" Diequest asked.

"Almost."

"Am I still in it?"

"It's all about you."

"Good, good. Very good." Diequest laughed. "I hope you didn't flatter me too much."

"It's called *The Wolf*."

"*The Wolf?*"

"Yes, a predator at sea."

"Well, Mr. London, maybe I'll read it"—Diequest laughed again—"if it ever gets printed."

"It'll get printed. I'll send you a copy. And I'll make sure the Maritime Court reads it, too. Bon voyage, Captain Diequest."

London threaded his way to the corner table and sat at the empty chair that Scratch pushed out.

"The Wolf?" Scratch squinted. "Is that what you think of him? I know there's bad blood between you—heard what happened when you landed. But he does pay the highest wages, brings in the most pelts, and—"

"Scratch," said London, taking hold of Nelson's thick arm, "you're not thinking of signing on with him?"

"Well, times is hard, Jack." Nelson looked at Maimie. "And I ain't anxious to lift anchor, but I *am* a sailor, and things being such as they are, I thought—"

"Scratch, listen to me. I don't care how hard times are—if you have to eat snails and cats and rats, if you have to steal from the poor box or mug ministers—just promise me you'll never sign on with Diequest. Slug a copper and do time in San Quentin"—he looked at Maimie—"but, Maimie, don't ever let him ship out with that murdering son of a bitch." He turned back to Nelson. "Scratch, do you hear what I'm saying?"

"All right, Jack." Nelson nodded. "I hear you."

Captain Diequest also heard.

In spite of Scratch's importunings to "stick around and yarn about the good ol' days," Jack decided not to get pipped. He drank his beer, bade Maimie and Scratch goodbye, and walked past Diequest.

He went home that afternoon, took a bath, and slept for twenty-four hours. When he arose, he went into the kitchen, fried himself a beefsteak and a pan of potatoes, sliced three tomatoes, and ate as if it were his last meal.

It turned out to be the last meal he would eat until he finished his novel.

Forty-eight hours later, he wrote the final words of the final chapter: *And the sea shall give up the dead which are in it; and death and hell deliver up the dead which are in them: and they will be judged every man according to their works. Amen.*

Then London went back to the beginning and wrote the dedication:

*For Elmer Dodson
who taught*

◁ CHAPTER 23 ▷

A BLEAK, OVERCAST summer sky shrouded the bay, presaging the storm that would surely come. The air was thick and moist, the sun a distant leaden circle.

Jack and Felicity walked toward the oak tree. He had brought the manuscript with him. When they sat, he placed it in her lap.

"It's finished."

"Oh, Jack, it *will* be published. I know it will. Philip said he'd do everything he could to help. But it would be published even without Philip. You'll be successful and famous and—"

"And we'll live happily ever after, isn't that the way it's supposed to be?"

"I hope so, Jack. I dearly hope so." She touched his face. "Jack, Mother knows about us—the letters, our Sunday meetings—she's found out everything."

"I guess she was bound to."

"We had a long talk, and I must admit she said some terrible things at first."

"I can imagine how she felt about her daughter being with someone so beneath the Bambridges."

"You don't understand her, Jack. She only wants what's best for me—"

"So do I."

"She told me things about herself that I could never have conceived, things that . . . well, never mind. The important thing is that I've convinced her to see you again, to talk to you and get to know you better."

"I'm not so sure that will help our cause."

"Don't joke about it, Jack. She wants you to come to the house tonight, at six. We're making progress. Will you do it, will you come? You must!"

"On one condition," he said, and smiled.

"And what is that?"

"That you read at least part of the book first. Will you do it? You must!" He repeated her words and tone.

"You've struck a bargain." Felicity smiled back.

"I . . . I dedicated it to Mr. Dodson," he said with some apprehension.

"I think that would have made him very happy." Her voice was sincere and even proud.

Jack lay on the grass and slept while Felicity read. He awoke two hours later and saw that she was halfway through the manuscript, but staring straight at him, her body rigid, her face pale and uneasy.

"You don't think it's any good," he said as he sat up.

"I . . . I've never read anything like it."

"But you don't think it's any good!"

"Jack, who's going to want—or pay to read something so shocking, so brutal?"

"Never mind."

"You don't expect women to read something like this? Jack, darling, it's vulgar and savage."

"That's the world and what's in it."

"Whose world? Not mine . . . not ours."

"We're a part of the same world, each and every one, and each accountable for everything that's in it. Felicity, you've never been south of the Slot. The world is not all made up of soft fat people eating out of sterling settings in velvet rooms and sleeping on soft, warm beds and goosefeathers.

"When I was eight years old, I stole a piece of meat from a kid in school—a piece of meat no bigger than these two fingers—because I was hungry. Have you ever been hungry, Felicity? Not supper-is-an-hour-late hungry, but hungry like half the world is. Hungry enough to beg, or steal, or hurt—hungry enough to want to blow somebody's brains out . . . or maybe your own? Have you?"

"No, Jack!" She pulled away. "I haven't, thank God I haven't! And I don't want to hear about it—or read about it!"

"All right." He rose to his feet. "Don't hear about it, don't read about it, don't know about it—and don't *do* anything about it. And if everybody felt that way, nothing would ever change."

"Do you honestly think that you can change the world for the better?"

"I've changed myself, and that's a start."

"Yes! Yes, you have—and I love you for it. That's exactly what I said to Mother."

"You did? You told your mother that you loved me? Did you, Felicity?"

She thought for just a moment before she spoke.

"I . . . may not have used the words, but, Jack, she can't fail to understand my feelings. I told her how hard you've studied and worked to rise above adversity—that I knew you would succeed—"

"That was before you read the book."

"Put the book aside for now; maybe I'm not the one to evaluate its worth. But that has nothing to do with my evaluation or feeling or belief in you. Jack, fight with the world if you must, but please don't fight with me. . . . I'm just not made that way, I'm just not strong enough . . ." She began to sob.

He went to her, took the manuscript, put it on the ground,

and gently lifted her close to him. "Felicity, you're the last one in the world I want to fight with—I'm sorry I blew up."

He kissed her forehead, then her lips. "Am I forgiven?"

"Of course, but . . ." She nestled at his chest.

"But what?"

"Jack, when you're with Mother, please, please don't talk about stealing a piece of meat or people going hungry or—"

"No, no, I won't." He laughed and held her close again. "I promise you. I will be the very essence of elegance and good manners. Felicity, I will make you proud of me. I am going home and soap myself from stem to stern, break out a brand-new shirt, iron and put on my mended suit, brush up my brogans, and promptly at six arrive at the manor with a smile on my face. I will be carefree and charming and speak only of pleasantries. Nothing your mother says or does will remove that smile."

At one minute past six, Jack London, freshly scrubbed, wearing a new shirt under his mended suit, feet enclosed in unscuffed shoes, stepped into the Bambridge parlor with a smile on his face, as he followed a radiant Felicity.

He bowed from the waist and greeted Mrs. Bambridge, who sat gracefully in her usual chair.

"Good evening, Mrs. Bambridge."

Florence Bambridge never looked more regal and correct. She was flawlessly groomed and elegantly gowned. She looked as if she were a cameo, and just as cold. Her imperious voice wasted no words upon amenities.

"Mr. London, it was my daughter's wish that you and I meet again, and now that you are here, I do believe it would be wiser if I spoke to you alone."

Jack was caught off guard, and Felicity was startled at the words and tone of her mother's declaration.

"Mother, what are you saying? I thought—"

"Never mind what you thought. What I have to say to

Mr. London might be disquieting. You're not used to that sort of thing."

"I'm certainly not used to anything like this. Nobody is. But anything you have to say to Jack involves me. I'm staying." She took hold of London's hand and waited for her mother's reaction.

"Yes, it does involve you. But remember it was your decision. And remember one thing more, Felicity; some time ago I gave you fair warning that I would not tolerate this sort of thing."

"Excuse me, Mrs. Bambridge." Jack had recovered somewhat from the rude blow of her inhospitality—Hell, he thought to himself, hostility is the word. He decided, however, that he would be civil but not servile. "May I inquire what you mean by 'that sort of thing'?"

"Have you not, Mr. London, been writing love letters to my daughter?"

"They were not love letters, Mrs. Bambridge, and the correspondence was only on her side, since circumstances did not permit me to reply."

"No, but circumstances did permit you to skulk away with her on Sunday afternoons and make shameful advances in a public park and do your worst to sully her innocence. Do you deny that?"

"With due respect, Mrs. Bambridge, I deny everything except meeting with Felicity in the park—and that was only because you made it quite clear that I wasn't welcome here."

"Don't lie to me, Mr. London! You were observed—"

"Mother!"

"You were observed holding hands and caressing. Can you deny that?"

"No, ma'am. I can't and I don't. What's more, I won't try to deny how I feel about Felicity, but—"

"I presume, *Mr.* London, that you are about to assure me of your honorable intentions."

"Well, something like that," said London as Felicity held his hand even tighter.

"All the worse." Florence Bambridge rose and became an even more commanding figure. "I have but one daughter, and, like any concerned mother, I want that daughter to marry a gentleman. A man who is educated. A man who is cultured. A man who can provide for her comfort, and above all, a man who can give her an honorable name. You will agree that those are high standards."

"Mother." Felicity took a step forward, letting go of Jack's hand, "Let's not go over all—"

"Be quiet, Felicity, and listen. Now, Mr. London, shall we forego all the above requisites except the latter?"

"I don't know what you're getting at."

"You will, directly. And I'll be brief. Some time ago I engaged a Mr. Robert MacNamara. He's what is termed a private investigator."

"To do what?" London asked.

"Some 'research.'" Mrs. Bambridge stepped to a nearby table and picked up a folder. She opened it and glanced at the contents, several typewritten sheets of paper. "Your mother's maiden name was Flora Wellman. She has a scar across her forehead—"

"What has this got to do with Felicity and me?"

"Have the courtesy to let me finish, Mr. London—that *is* the name you go by?"

"It's my father's name," Jack answered quickly.

"Is it? I think not. And neither does Mr. MacNamara."

She held up some of the typewritten papers. "According to these records, mostly copies of newspaper articles, Miss Flora Wellman, your mother, was a well-known spiritualist—also an advocate of 'free love'—"

"Let me see that!"

"You are welcome to keep them when I finish . . . an advocate of 'free love,' who lived without benefit of marriage with one Professor William H. Chaney, an astrologist."

"Mother, please stop it!" Felicity shouted.

Philip Bambridge had stepped into the room but nobody noticed.

"You may leave whenever you choose, Felicity." Mrs. Bambridge referred to another sheet of paper. "From this relationship, an illegitimate son was born on the fourteenth of January, 1876. That *is* your birth date, is it not?"

"That's a lie! John London is my father!"

"Flora Wellman married John London on the seventh of September, 1876—nearly eight months *after* you were born, some time *after* she attempted suicide with a gun."

Florence Bambridge handed the folder to Jack. "As I said, you may keep this."

"Mother." Felicity looked from London to her mother and spoke with some of the same assurance and strength that Florence Bambridge had. "None of this makes any difference."

"Doesn't it?" Mrs. Bambridge declared.

"Damn you, Mother! Shut up!" Philip stepped forward and moved toward London. "Jack, I once apologized for my mother's rudeness. There can be no apology for the contemptible thing she's just done. But I promise you I'll do everything in my power to make up for it in any way I can. You have my solemn word."

Jack was numb. Without a word, he turned and walked out of the room, still holding the folder.

Felicity fell into a chair and wept. Philip went to her and put his arm around her shoulder as the front door closed.

◁ CHAPTER 24 ▷

HALF AN HOUR later, Jack London sat alone at a table at the Hatch. He had a bottle of whiskey in front of him and was reading a typewritten copy of an article from the *Chronicle*, dated June 4, 1875, with the banner: A DISCARDED WIFE—WHY MRS. CHANEY TWICE ATTEMPTED SUICIDE.

His eyes swept across what followed: *Driven from Home for Refusing to Destroy her Unborn Infant—A Chapter of Heartlessness and Domestic Misery.*

Day before yesterday Mrs. Chaney, wife of "Professor" W. H. Chaney, the astrologer, attempted suicide by taking laudanum. Failing in the effort she yesterday shot herself with a pistol in the forehead. The ball glanced off, inflicting only a flesh wound, and friends interfered before she could accomplish her suicidal purpose.

THE INCENTIVE TO THE TERRIBLE ACT

was domestic infelicity. Husband and wife have been known for a year past as the center of a little band of extreme Spiritualists, most of whom professed, if they did not practice, the offensive free-love doctrines of the licentious Woodhull . . . . Chaney practiced astrology, calculated horoscopes for a consideration, lectured on chemistry and astronomy, blasphemed the Christian religion, published a journal of hybrid doctrines, called the *Philomathean,* and pretended to calculate "cheap nativities" on the transit of the planets for $10 each . . .

THE WIFE'S DESPAIR AND ATTEMPTED SUICIDE

He then left her, and shortly afterwards she made her first attempt at suicide, following it by the effort to kill herself with a pistol on the following morning as already stated. Failing in both endeavors, Mrs. Chaney was removed in a half-insane condition from Dr. Ruttley's on Mission Street to the house of a friend, where she still remains, somewhat pacified and in a mental condition indicating that she will not again attempt self-destruction. The story given here is the lady's own, as filtered through her near associates.

London glanced at the notation added by Robert MacNamara: *The Chronicle was being gallant on behalf of the woman in question. In truth Flora Wellman and William Chaney were never married.*

He took another drink of whiskey and decided it was time to go home.

He took the bottle with him.

◁ CHAPTER 25 ▷

THE LONDON FAMILY was gathered in the gaslit parlor that Sunday evening—John, Flora, Eliza, and Jack. It had begun to rain heavily as Jack walked home from the Hatch with the whiskey bottle in his hand and the MacNamara folder tucked inside his shirt. It was still raining as he stood in front of Eliza and held the bottle in one hand, the typewritten sheets from the folder in the other.

"An awful lot to take aboard in one day . . . to find that my sister is not my sister . . ." He turned and moved a step toward John London, who sat in a rocker, his face drawn and tormented. "That my father's not my father . . ." Jack wheeled toward Flora, the only one in the room who remained calm and impassive. She was still strong and straight, and looked directly at her son.

"And that my mother—my mother . . ."—the word was brine in his throat. He took a drink from the bottle. ". . . an awful lot to take aboard in one day."

"Jack." John London spoke barely above a whisper. "To me, you are my son."

"I know." Jack replied with great affection. "I know that, and I couldn't have asked for a better father."

Then London looked to his mother, whose gaze locked with his. He walked close to her.

"But what am I to the man Chaney? *Chaney—Chaney.* No, I might have been born Jack Chaney, but I'll die Jack London. And where is this Professor William H. Chaney? Is he dead? Is he alive? Has he sired a string of other bastards like me? With other women like—"

Flora slapped him hard across the mouth. "Your mother? That's right, Jack. No matter what you think of me, I am your mother. But Chaney didn't want a son—he wanted me to kill you before you were born. At first I wanted to kill myself. I even tried. But then I said, To hell with him—it was him or you, and I chose you—To hell with what people would think. I'd live! And so would you! And you'd grow up to be a man!"

She paused for just a moment but lost no mettle. "I don't know if he's alive or dead, and I don't give a damn. So don't look at me like that. I've lived with it for half my life. We all have. And if you can't live with it now . . . to hell with you, too!"

Flora London turned and walked out of the room. No one spoke. Eliza went over to Jack. She kissed him.

London lay awake most of the night listening to the rain, his mind swirling with images of himself from infancy to manhood—of his mother, Eliza, John London, and the faceless William H. Chaney. Mammy Jenny must have known and kept the secret. Now others knew. Felicity, Mrs. Bambridge, Philip—how many others?

He knew that he had lost Felicity. What else had he lost?

The rain stopped. He fell asleep just before dawn.

When Jack awoke, it was past noon. He dressed, went to the bathroom, brushed his teeth, scooped cold water on his face, and thought to himself that for the first time since coming home he was neither writing nor working. It was a vacuous feeling. Then he thought about coffee.

The family had already had dinner. John sat in the rocker in the parlor, and Flora and Eliza were still in the kitchen.

As Jack walked down the stairs, someone twisted the knob on the front doorbell.

"I'll get it," Jack said to Eliza as she started from the kitchen.

When Jack opened the door, he saw a pleasant-faced, somewhat portly middle-aged man. He was well dressed in a conservative manner and might have been a lawyer or professor, except for his too-cheerful smile. Salesman, Jack quickly appraised.

"Good afternoon," the man greeted. "My name is Quincy, Myron Quincy. May I speak to Mr. London?"

"Which Mr. London?" Jack inquired.

"Mr. London the writer. Jack London."

"I'm Jack London."

"Yes"—Quincy's smile widened as his eyes assessed the breadth of London's shoulders—"I might have guessed. You certainly fit the description. May I come in?"

Jack nodded. Mr. Quincy entered and extended his hand. "Young man, I've heard a great deal about you."

"Who from?" Jack asked as they shook hands.

"A good friend of yours." Quincy winked. "I promised I wouldn't mention any names. I represent a publishing house in the East—Boston." He produced a card from his vest pocket and presented it to London.

"Oh, Mr. Quincy, this is my family." Flora and Eliza had come in from the kitchen at the sound of the man's voice.

"Delighted." Quincy beamed.

"Olympic Publications," Jack read the card.

"Yes. Frankly, we're interested in works of adventure. Think it's the coming market. That's why I'm here to see you."

John and Eliza were entranced. Even Flora reacted.

"You didn't come all the way from Boston just to see me, did you, Mr. Quincy?"

"No, no. Happened to be in town on company business when I heard about you and your book."

"This 'good friend' . . . Philip Bambridge?"

"Now, Mr. London," Quincy all but confessed to Jack's deduction. "A promise is a promise. Is there somewhere we can talk . . . about your book?"

"The book. . . . Yes, yes, there sure is, Mr. Quincy. Why don't we go upstairs where I wrote it?"

"That sounds . . . appropriate." Quincy laughed.

Myron Quincy was not laughing half an hour later as he sat in London's swivel chair with the manuscript and diary open on the rolltop desk before him.

"And such a man as this Captain Diequest actually exists?"

Jack nodded.

"Amazing! Of course, I've only read a few passages, but I think it's just what we're looking for. Yes, sir, Mr. London. This just might cause quite a sensation in literary circles. I'd like to take a copy with me and—"

"You mean, to Boston?"

"Well, eventually, yes, I certainly hope so." Quincy smiled broadly. "But for the time being, just to my hotel room. Stopping off at a charming little place called the White Dolphin, near the waterfront. I'll make it my business to finish reading the manuscript by sometime this evening."

"If you do accept, Mr. Quincy, how long before I'd get any money?"

"Immediately. Just as soon as you sign the contract, I'm authorized to make the advance payment of five hundred dollars. I'd like to look over the diary, too—might have some suggestions, if you don't mind?"

"No, I don't . . . five hundred . . . certainly not, but . . ." Jack glanced at the manuscript.

"What is it? Are the terms not satisfactory?"

"Oh no, sir, they're satisfactory, all right. It's just that those"—Jack pointed to the manuscript and diary—"are my only copies."

"I see." Quincy rubbed his chin and reflected. "I'll be leaving town Thursday, and I suppose we could get it retyped, but that would take—"

"You go ahead and take them, Mr. Quincy. I'm anxious for you to read them just as soon as possible, and for me to sign that contract if you still want to publish *The Wolf*."

"I don't think there's much doubt about that, Mr. London—and we will have another copy typed for you to keep. In the meanwhile, I promise you these are in safe hands." Quincy rose. "Shall I contact you here?"

"Uh, no, sir. Tonight I'll be at the Hatch, and if we make the deal, I'm going over to wake up Philip even if it's two o'clock in the morning—and I hope his mother answers the door."

"I'm afraid you've lost me, young man," Quincy laughed and tugged at his ear, "somewhere around the Hatch. What is the Hatch?"

"It's a bar—I'll write down the address." Jack took a pencil and wrote across the front page of the diary.

"Excellent." Myron Quincy beamed. "You'll hear from me tonight sometime after supper."

◁ CHAPTER 26 ▷

At ten fifteen that night, there was eighty-seven cents inside the tin cup pinned to the empty pantleg of Misery, who squeezed music out of his accordion in the Hatch. A couple of card games were in progress, a few sailors at the bar, and three well-worn women present.

Jack London sat alone at a table with a nearly half-empty bottle of whiskey in front of him. He turned Myron Quincy's card over and over in his hand. By now Quincy must almost be finished reading *The Wolf*, and Jack London's future, or at least his immediately foreseeable future, hinged on this stranger's reaction. He had certainly liked what he read well enough. After Mr. Quincy left, Jack told his family what had transpired upstairs. John London wept. Eliza threw her arms around him and kissed him, and Flora said she would believe it all when she saw the money "in cash . . . not a check. Coin of the realm."

All day and into the night, Jack kept wishing he had the power to make time go faster. Instead, every hour, every minute, snailed.

Jack had placed Mr. Dodson's gold-filled watch and chain in a drawer for safekeeping, but he still carried the dollar pocket watch he'd had for years. The hands of that watch seemed unwilling to move. His stomach rejected the notion of food, and his brain raced at the prospect of publication and money. He dared to think even of Felicity again. But he would not allow his hopes where Felicity was concerned to go too far, too fast. There was still Mrs. Bambridge to cross. But Philip! Good old Philip had been better than his word.

As London looked at his watch again, the front door opened and Maimie stood framed against the fog. Jack was surprised to see her unescorted. Maimie paused only a beat before walking in with that pulsating movement of her pliant body. She wore only a sheer, pale blue summer skirt and blouse dampened from the fog and clinging in revelation of her every contour. Maimie moistened her lips, smiled, and moved with unmistakable intent toward London.

"Hello, Jack," she purred. "I said I'd see you around."

London poured himself another drink and couldn't help noticing how the sheer damp blouse cohered to her breasts.

"Hello, Maimie. Where's Scratch?"

She made the most of a shrug. "We had a fight. The big dumb Swede sonofabitch." Maimie looked from London to the bottle. "You, too?" She laughed. "Ain't that rich? How about buying me a drink . . . to old times?"

"Why not? Get yourself a glass."

"I'll just do that." She walked to the bar in a way that made Jack momentarily forget that he was awaiting word from Myron Quincy.

She came back and sat with legs wide apart, pulling the chair close to London as he dipped the bottle at both glasses.

"Ain't seen you take on anything this hard for a long time." She downed the drink in a smooth single swallow and set the glass on the table, indicating more.

London shrugged as he poured. "Hard times call for hard . . . beverages."

"Yeah. Damn, that fog always makes me thirsty . . . and you remember what else, Jack."

He remembered but didn't answer.

"What's the matter, Jack—the little lady think she's too good for you?" Maimie teased. "Well, I know what's good for you, and she can't—"

"Shut up about her, Maimie. Just drink your drink and shut up about her."

"Aw, Jack, I didn't mean nothing. Hell, you know—"

"I know." He nodded. "I'm sorry."

"Will you show me *how* sorry?" Her voice was soothing and seductive. "We've got all night."

"No, Maimie, I'm trawled toward the temptation, but I have a previous engagement."

"With her? She's too skinny for you, Jack, why there ain't enough meat on her to—"

"Not with her. With truth." He lifted his glass. "Maimie, here's to truth. As the poet put it, 'Bitter, barren, truth.' "

"What're you talking about?"

"How does it go?" London rubbed his forehead. "Oh, yes . . .

" 'Give me the glorious dreams that
   fooled me in my youth,
The sweet mirage that lured me
   to my fate.
And take away the bitter, barren truth . . .' "

He looked at Quincy's card and finished the quotation: " 'Success I fear has come too late.' "

"What do you mean, 'too late'? Hell, Jack, you're younger than I am."

London took another drink. "Maimie, I'm as old as the Bar Sinister."

"The Bar Sinister? Where's that? That's one joint I never heard of. Jack, for somebody who's read as many books as you, you're not making much sense."

A young fellow sixteen or seventeen, thin, with yellow

hair wildly protruding beneath a sailor's stocking cap, and with green eyes, and pocked complexion, entered the Hatch. He walked over to the bar, spoke with Baldy, then approached London's table. As he came closer, he became more and more fascinated by the face and figure of Maimie.

"Excuse me," the young fellow cleared his throat. He flicked another glance at Maimie and back to Jack. "Mr. London?"

"*Mister* London." Jack smiled and nodded. "That's I—a fact, an irrefragable fact."

The young fellow was again looking at Maimie, who made a slight motion with her shoulders so that her breasts reacted in accommodation. She knew exactly what she was doing. The young man swallowed and pulled an envelope out of his pea coat.

"I . . . I was asked to bring this to you, Mr. London." He managed to hand an envelope to Jack.

"Mister London thanks you." Jack started to reach into his pocket. "Just a minute."

"It's all been taken care of . . . thanks." The young fellow backed away, savoring a last lingering appraisal of Maimie. "It's been nice to have met you, ma'am."

"Likewise." Maimie smiled and made another shoulder adjustment.

London tore the envelope open and read the brief note.

"Say, Jack," Maimie inquired, "how did Green Eyes know where to find you?"

"Because I am famous, Maimie. Listen." Jack read:

" 'Dear Jack: I think *The Wolf* is excellent. Waiting at the White Dolphin Hotel, Two Hundred Beacon St., Room Nineteen, to conclude our deal. Please come by immediately. Myron Quincy.'

"And never sweeter words were written, Maimie, my friend."

"What kind of a deal you gonna 'conclude' at this time of night?"

"You'll see. They'll all see. Big . . . very big deal. The biggest deal that was ever made during this dear ol' waning century." He started to rise but was somewhat unsteady. The lack of food and excess whiskey had affected him more than he had realized.

"Well, whatever it is, and wherever it is—I'm going with you," she said. "You could use a rudder."

"Sure, Maimie. Why not? You be my rudder. Steer me toward the White Dolphin Hotel."

London walked to the bar and set the whiskey bottle on top.

"Baldy, you store this bottle. We'll be back to celebrate." Jack dropped a quarter in Misery's tin cup, crooked his left elbow for Maimie to slip her arm through, and headed for the door.

The streets were sparsely populated. The yellow gas lamps flickered through the yeasty fog filtering in from the bay. In the distance, a ship's whistle moaned and was given shrill answer by a smaller boat.

Two sailors stood smoking in the doorway of a closed grocery store—large, ugly, grim men who might have been brothers. Both had beetled brows, piggish eyes, and exaggerated jaws. The sailors peered at Jack and Maimie as they approached, particularly at Maimie, who squeezed a warning into Jack's arm. But he was already aware of the watchers.

"Evenin', mates," London said in a strong, clear voice, even though he still felt somewhat unsteady from the drink.

There was no answer. Maimie did her best to walk as unseductively as she could. There wasn't too much she could do, given the equipment she possessed. London's right hand had turned into a ready fist anticipating the slightest movement from the sailors. But the sailors looked quickly at each other and by some unseen signal decided to make no move, if that was what they had intended in the first place.

"Did you see the mugs on them two gorillas?" Maimie

said once they were out of earshot. "Didn't think two men could be so ugly. Makes a girl appreciate a strong, handsome escort all the more."

"Thanks, Maimie." Jack smiled. "I'm a pretty good singer, too. Just listen to this . . ." He started to sing, making up his own lyrics to the old English ditty 'A Capital Ship':

So blow ye winds hi-ho
A rovin' we will go
I'll stay no more
On Oakland's shore
I'm a rich son of a—
Gun, I am, I am . . .

Maimie pulled Jack to a stop. He looked at her. "What's the matter? Don't you like my singing?"

She pointed across the street through the murky fog to a sign that was barely visible: *White Dolphin Hotel.*

"We made it." Jack grinned. "You're a good rudder, Maimie, old girl, old pearl—a good rudder."

Jack and Maimie entered the hotel. The lobby was quiet and clean, with a red velvet couch encircling a large post in the middle of the room. Other than that, the place looked almost like a men's club. There were several deep leather wingback chairs, a fireplace, and seascapes on the walls. A slight, bespectacled man with an old woman's face sat bent behind the desk reading a magazine. He looked condescendingly at Jack and Maimie as they approached. He seemed particularly to deplore Maimie's presence.

"Good evening," Jack cheerfully declared. "Good evening."

"I'm sure it is," the clerk responded in an effeminate voice and nervous, mincing manner. "But I'm sorry, young man, all our rooms are occupied."

"My congratulations," Jack replied. "One of those rooms,

number nineteen, is occupied by Mr. Quincy. He's expecting me. Jack London."

"Oh, yes, yes, Mr. London." The clerk made a bit of a fuss over some papers on the desk, sorting and straightening and then setting them back precisely as they had been. "Mr. Quincy *is* in room nineteen."

"Verily, verily." Jack nodded and winked at Maimie with great confidence.

"Straight down the hall, sir. The room nearest the window and on your left, sir."

"Many thanks," said Jack, starting toward the hall.

"But I'm afraid the . . ."—the clerk's voice and manner took on an even more feminine tone—"lady . . . will have to wait in the lobby. Hotel policy."

"Very proper, very proper." Jack escorted Maimie toward the circular red velvet couch. "Maimie, you sit down and I'll be back with the booty."

"Jack," Maimie whispered. "You all right?"

"Ship . . . shape." Jack patted her hand as she sat. "Ship—shape."

Maimie adjusted her skirt and watched as Jack walked into the narrow hallway. The clerk lost none of his condescension or contempt as he looked back over his shoulder at the blond, blue-eyed girl in the too-tight skirt and blouse, with extraordinarily long legs, sitting on the circular red velvet couch.

London walked almost to the end of the hallway, looking at the numbers on the doors to his left. Thirteen. Fifteen. Seventeen. Nineteen. He adjusted his coat, ran his fingers through his damp, ruffled hair, and knocked.

"Come." A muffled voice responded from inside.

Jack opened the door and entered. It was strangely dark, but a figure sitting at a chair behind a desk was discernible. On the desk was a lamp, but turned low, barely illuminating the silhouette.

As London stepped in, the door behind him slammed shut and two other shadows blocked the door.

The figure at the chair was already reaching over and turning up the lamp.

"What the hell is this?" Jack said.

Erik Diequest took his peaked cap from the desk and placed it squarely on his head.

"At the moment it is the captains's cabin." Diequest smiled. "Welcome aboard, Mr. London."

Suddenly, Jack had never been so sober. He looked behind him. There stood Spinner and Cookie, human barricades at the door. Each man had a sinister smile on his face and a sap in his hand.

"I see you did finish the last chapter." Diequest pointed at the manuscript and diary tied together with string and placed on top of the desk. "It was a very ambitious undertaking. I'm sure you labored long and hard."

"Then Mr. Quincy isn't—"

"No." Diequest smiled. "Mr. Quincy isn't a representative of a publishing house in Boston. I'm afraid he isn't even Mr. Quincy. Name's Farnsworth, or so he claims. Carnival man—among other things—has sold bibles, diamond mines, cemetery plots, fertile farmland that has somehow sunk beneath the sea. An amiable confidence man, an artist really."

"And there is no Olympic Publications . . ."

"Who think 'works of adventure are the coming market' ? Mr. London, for three dollars you can have enough cards like that printed to flood the city. But of course, you were too anxious, greedy, and egocentric to do any checking. All that is part of the confidence game, or so Mr. Farnsworth assured me. Obviously, he knew how to sell the butcher his own meat."

Maimie adjusted her skirt again, looked down the hallway, then at the clerk, who checked the time from the dainty silver pocket watch that was connected to a slim silver chain threaded through a notch in his double-breasted lapel, replaced the watch in his breast pocket, left the desk, and went out of a door at the rear of the room.

In a moment Maimie rose and walked over to look too closely at a painting on the wall. While she was at it she pulled the curtain of a window aside and looked into the alley.

The fidgety clerk was just outside the alley door waving at something or someone in the distance. Out of the fog a wagon appeared.

Maimie walked quickly across the lobby into the hallway toward room nineteen.

"Mr. London, I did enjoy reading what you wrote about me, although in my opinion you set down purple prose with a lavish hand. You've a strong flare for words but are afflicted with a terminal disease—a kinship for the weak and frail. You lack the instinct of the ape and tiger for survival. And that, among other failings, I'm afraid, dooms you to premature extinction."

"I suppose I can consider that my first review," London said. "Of course, your point of view is somewhat prejudiced."

"Your first and *last* review, Mr. London. It's a pity, but nobody else is ever going to read it. I have plans for this—material. Those plans do not include publication." Diequest tapped the manuscript. "I'm told there are no other copies."

"You're wrong. There's another copy." London touched his forehead. "Here."

"Ahh yes. But the human mind can be so unstable." Diequest held up the manuscript and diary. "An awful lot of words to remember."

"I'll remember."

"We shall see." Diequest smiled. "but first—"

London spun abruptly, hit Cookie in the jaw, and made for the doorknob. Spinner's sap came down hard at London who moved his head aside and took the vicious blow on his shoulder.

Cookie came to his feet, and he and Spinner attacked London from both sides.

Diequest lit a cigar.

London managed to knock Cookie down again, but Spinner's sap struck Jack across the head, pitching him onto a table. The table, a vase on top of it, and London all crashed onto the floor.

"The son of a bitch," muttered Spinner as he pumped for breath, "ain't easy to make fall."

"Lift him up," Diequest commanded.

Spinner and Cookie, who had pretty well recovered, pulled London to his feet. As Jack came to, his captors twisted both arms behind him. Diequest rose, exhaled a circle of blue smoke, and came close.

"I was about to say that first you need something to clear your head, Mr. London." Diequest was obviously enjoying the cigar and the situation. "A long sea voyage ought to do it."

"You can't get away with shanghaiing me, Diequest."

"Can't I?"

Maimie was outside in the hallway. She had heard the blows and noise of the fight and now stooped with her ear pressed against the keyhole. She could distinctly hear Diequest's triumphant voice.

"The *North Star*'s in the harbor waiting for the tide. And there's a jollyboat at the pier . . . waiting just for us. Oh, it's been done before Mr. London, many times and it'll be done again tonight. To you."

Maimie rose and hurried to the window at the end of the hall. It took her less than five seconds to open it, crawl through, and hit the street running.

"Even if you get me aboard the *North Star*," London said as Spinner and Cookie still gripped him, "sooner or later the voyage'll end. . . ."

"Yes, the voyage will end, Mr. London, And you'll be just one more sailor"—Diequest's right fist pounded into Jack's stomach—"lost at sea." Then his fist crashed into London's jaw.

There was soft tapping at the door.

"Are you ready?" the clerk's unctuous voice inquired.

"We're ready," Diequest replied.

Spinner and Cookie carried the unconscious London, gagged and with hands tied behind him, out the rear door to the wagon and driver waiting in the damp, dark alley. Diequest carried the manuscript and diary in one hand, his cigar in the other.

The two men tossed London onto the bed of the wagon and climbed aboard.

"I don't know where the . . . girl went, Captain," the clerk fluttered. "She was obviously one of those . . . women of the street."

"Maybe she went out looking for better company," Diequest said, and reached into his pocket. "It doesn't matter. Here's your fee, Mr. Beasly. Thank you and good night."

"Thank *you*, Captain," Mr. Beasly bubbled. "I'm happy to be of service to you anytime."

"Yes," Diequest grunted, and climbed up next to the driver. "Move."

The driver nodded and snapped the reins ribboned through his fingers. The two animals responded, pulling the wagon through the cobblestoned alley toward the fog-gloomed street.

◁ CHAPTER 27 ▷

THE DOOR TO the Hatch flew open. Maimie ran through and looked around. Baldy was washing glasses. Misery had departed, and so had most of the customers. But Scratch sat at a table with three other men, playing poker and drinking. Maimie recognized the dealer, Joe Goose, who looked just like his name. She didn't know the other two.

Maimie raced toward Scratch. Her hair was wet and disheveled, and she held her side where it hurt from running. She was drained of energy and breath. "Scratch, Jack's in trouble! Bad trouble!"

"Good for him." Scratch looked up calmly, then back to the dealer. "One card, Goose."

Joe Goose dealt a card.

"Scratch! Damn you!" Maimie grabbed Nelson's shoulder. "Listen to me!"

"Get yer clams off me. I heard you two left together."

"He was drunk! I was just trying to—"

"Yeah, I know what you was trying to do. You been trying to do it ever since he got back. Well, you finally got him, and you're welcome to keep him." Nelson looked at Joe Goose. "Are we playin' cards here?"

"Listen to me, Scratch!" Maimie persisted. "Diequest's shanghaiing him!"

"What do I care? Go to the coppers with your sad story."

"The cops aren't gonna listen to me! They don't give a damn."

"Neither do I. Goose, are you gonna deal?"

"London was always on the square," Joe Goose said. "He's pulled me outa a squeeze more'n once."

"Sure he has," Maimie pleaded. "Scratch, there ain't much time—you gotta help him!"

"Why should I?"

"Because he warned you about Diequest. Because he'd help you. Because he's one of us!"

◁ CHAPTER 28 ▷

London lay face down. His eyes opened, but he did not move.

He tried to obliterate the maggots from his mind and determine what had happened after Diequest struck, and where he was now lying. Slowly, things came into focus and he pieced together the circumstances and geography. He was in a moving wagon. Tied and gagged. He turned his head slightly and caught sight of Spinner and Cookie. The wagon was nearing the waterfront. The night sounds of the sea were getting louder against the plopping of the horses' hooves and the creaking of the wagon.

It had all been for nothing. Diequest had won. He had the manuscript. All the time and effort Jack had put into it—for nothing. The deprivation, the drudgery of the endless days, the nightly battles to stay awake and write—for nothing.

All that time Diequest had watched and waited, sleeping in comfort, filling his belly, smoking his cigars, and planning his devious little drama with the confidence man, Farnsworth. And Jack had taken the bait as Farnsworth knew he would. Not checking Quincy's credentials or finding out if Olympic existed, lulled by the confidence in himself and the coincidence of Philip's promise. Perhaps Philip would have helped Jack to get the book published. He would have tried. But it was too late now.

In a few minutes they would be in the jollyboat and on their way to the hell ship ruled by Diequest. London would lose more than the manuscript. Diequest would not resort to murder on dry land. But on the *North Star,* anything could happen. Anything that Diequest wanted.

London lifted his head a little higher, but Spinner shoved Jack's skull against the wagon and dangled the sap inches from Jack's face.

"You try anything again—you just make me think you're going to, and I'll splatter your brains all over this wagon." Spinner laughed and looked at Cookie. "He looks real nice down there, don't he, Cookie—just like a pig all strung up for slaughter."

"Shut up back there," Diequest's voice commanded through the fog. He put a fresh cigar into his mouth and struck a match with his thumbnail.

The water slapped against the pilings of the pier. A jollyboat was tied up alongside. Two sailors stood on the wooden wharf and smoked, one a cigarette, the other a pipe.

"What time is it?" one of the sailors asked.

"What do you care? You ain't going anyplace till they get here."

"You're right, I . . . listen!"

Out of the fog they heard the sound of horses' hooves on the timbers of the pier, the creaking and jangling of a wagon, then the moving outline forming through the haze.

"Captain, that you?" the sailor's voice called out.

"Yeah," Diequest shot back.

"Got him?"

"Got him."

The wagon rattled and groaned to a stop as the driver set the brake.

"Need a hand, Captain?" the sailor with the pipe asked.

"No," said Diequest. "You two make ready to cast off. We'll bring him along."

The two sailors who had waited turned and walked back toward the boat. Diequest jumped down from the wagon.

"All right, Mr. Spinner, set him to his feet and get him down here."

"Aye, sir." Spinner and Cookie pulled London upright in the wagon, and Jack saw Diequest for the first time since the captain had struck him. He now held the manuscript with that same hand.

"Make lively, Mr. London," Diequest said. "This is the last dry land you'll ever set foot on—"

The captain was interrupted by the sounds of wild yelling and screaming as another wagon pulled by two pounding horses careened around a corner, with slippery wheels sliding, bouncing off the ground and onto the wharf. The foaming horses snorted, with vapor steaming from their nostrils as Scratch Nelson, reins in one hand, whip in the other, snapped the lash across the animals' backs and charged straight for Diequest and the first wagon, with London, Spinner, Cookie, and the driver still aboard.

A radiantly happy Maimie sat next to Scratch, with Joe Goose and two allies right behind, standing in the wagon screaming like wild Apaches.

The charging horses, eyes ablaze, were almost upon Diequest as he leaped to the left. Scratch pulled his reins hard to the right, and the frenzied horses responded. But the hurtling wagon skidded across the sleek, moist wharf and smashed broadside into the stationary wagon. London, Spinner, Cookie, and the driver, along with Scratch, Maimie, Joe Goose, and the two allies were all pitched into the air and onto the pier.

Horses tore their traces and galloped off. The wagons were both overturned, wheels spinning.

Maimie and the men were doing their best to stagger to their feet and senses. The driver of the shanghai wagon was the first to succeed. He followed the horses' example and ran away.

Jack managed to roll from under the inverted wagon and almost fell into the bay. He spat the gag out of his mouth.

Diequest was on his knees and rising until Scratch Nelson landed like a flying bull on top of him.

The two sailors who had waited by the boat rushed to the aid of their captain and shipmates.

The confederates from both sides converged and exploded with fists, elbows, feet, saps, brass knuckles, and anything loose that could be picked up.

The brass knuckles were Joe Goose's specialty.

Scratch clubbed his fist into Diequest's face, knocking the captain against the overturned wagon. Nelson whipped out his knife, thumbed the lever, and the blade snapped open.

"Scratch," called London as he rolled onto his stomach. "Over here! Cut me loose!"

Scratch smiled a broad Scandinavian smile, leaned down, and slashed London free with one stroke.

"About Maimie." Scratch grinned.

"She's all yours." Jack made it to his feet, also grinning. "If she wants you."

"I'll take him." Maimie, with her nose bleeding, grabbed the spoke of a broken wagon wheel and swung it with both hands like a baseball bat across the head of a sailor who stalked Joe Goose.

London leaped for Diequest, who was ready. They fought as they had fought before, each with the fury of ape and tiger, slamming into each other, tearing at each other's throats, pounding into each other's body.

Scratch Nelson fell victim to a blow at the ear from Cookie. Then Cyrus Spinner got hold of a heavy board and broke it across London's back. He went down.

Spinner and Cookie helped Diequest get his bearings.

"We better get outa here, Captain," Spinner advised.

"Let's go," Diequest nodded.

London and his allies were all down—all but Maimie. She was on one knee, her pale blue summer dress dirty and tattered, one of her magnificent breasts exposed.

As Diequest and his crew moved off, the captain spotted the manuscript and diary still tied together on the wharf near an overturned wagon. He picked up the bundle and made for the jollyboat with his men.

Maimie screamed and ran toward Diequest. "Gimme that back, you sonofabitch!" she shrieked.

She clawed at Diequest, who viciously backhanded her onto the wharf.

London teetered to his knees, then pulled himself onto both feet. He saw Maimie lying face down on the pier and ran to her.

"Maimie!" He turned her over.

"Jack," she managed out of a swollen, bleeding mouth, "the book."

The jollyboat pulled away from the pier, with Diequest standing, while Spinner, Cookie, and the two others rowed for all their worth.

"*Lon-don!*" Diequest's voice cut through the night. He held up the manuscript.

London ran the length of the wharf and stopped at the edge just short of falling off. He could barely make out the silhouette of the captain as the boat drew farther away.

"*Lon-don!*" Diequest held up the bundled manuscript and diary and laughed. "Here's your precious manuscript. You want it? Come and get it!"

Diequest threw it as far as he could into the black, cold crypt of the sea.

Jack heard the splash and stared straight out until the jollyboat was swallowed by the fog, with Diequest still laughing.

◁ CHAPTER 29 ▷

GOLD! GOLD! GOLD!
IN ALASKA
Millionaires Made In
First Diggings

Sᴛᴏʀɪᴇs ᴏғ ᴛʜᴇ strike were bannered in headlines on every newspaper from San Francisco to New York. The *S.S. Excelsior* had entered the Golden Gate and anchored in San Francisco. The first millionaires from the gold strike in the Klondike stepped off the ship and infected the entire country with an epidemic of gold fever.

Not since Sutter's Mill had such madness spread across the land and sea. People who had never held a pick, who wouldn't know gold if they walked on it, who had never seen an icicle sought the solution to all their ills. GOLD! GOLD! GOLD! Waiting in Alaska to be carted off by the barrel, or so the stories went. And with them went the schemers, the crooks, the whores, the con men, the builders, the dreamers, and the adventurers.

Jack London had bought a ticket as passenger aboard the *Umatilla* of the Pacific Steamship Company. The *Umatilla* was built to carry two hundred and eighty passengers. Four hundred and seventy tickets had been sold at twenty-five dollars a fare from San Francisco to Juneau.

That morning in the London parlor, Jack, Flora, Eliza, John, and Mammy Jenny were gathered. Jack wore his seaman's outfit. His seabag leaned against a chair. Jack was putting money into Flora's hand.

"This'll have to tide you over, Mom, till I can send you more."

"Jack, where'd you get the money? You didn't do something wrong?"

"No, Mom, I didn't do anything wrong. And if I ever said anything wrong to you, I'm . . . sorry." Jack looked at Mammy Jenny, who avoided his glance. "I got the money from a friend. But I'll pay it back."

"Jack." Flora spoke to her son more tenderly than she ever had before. "I hope you're not just running away from us."

London shook his head and kissed his mother. He turned to John London, who rose from a chair with the aid of his cane.

"Dad." Jack embraced his father.

"I'll pray for you, son."

"I know you will." In his heart, Jack also knew that he was seeing his father for the last time.

London went to Mammy Jenny. She put her arms around him. "I hear it's awful cold up there in Alaska. You dress warm, baby."

"Thanks, Mammy Jenny." Jack nodded.

He lifted up the seabag and headed for the doorway, where Eliza waited. Her eyes were brimming as she placed both hands on Jack's face and kissed him.

"So long, sweet sister." He smiled and threw the seabag over his shoulder.

Jack London walked with the crowd toward the *Umatilla*. The pier was like a carnival, covered with people laughing, hugging, kissing and talking to each other, some in English but others in Italian, Greek, French, and Spanish. Those hearty, chesty men all going north to Alaska—all hoping to become millionaires. For most it was a false hope. Half would turn back on the journey from Juneau to Chilcoot Pass. Many of the others wouldn't last three months. Not even one percent of them would ever find gold. And the more who went, the less the chance. Still, as they started off, everyone had the same dream and thought he had the same chance aboard the *Umatilla*.

But Jack was thinking of another ship, the *North Star*, and her captain. Diequest had succeeded in destroying Jack's book—or at least this version of it. London could never sit down now and write it all again. It was too soon. But Diequest had not destroyed Jack London.

"Jack." It was Felicity's voice.

She stood near a carriage at the wharf. Philip sat in the driver's seat.

London walked through the crowd toward her. He nodded at Philip, who smiled and nodded back. Felicity came toward him and guided Jack to the rear of the carriage. They remained silent for a moment.

"Philip told me you were going to Alaska . . . to look for gold."

"That's not what I'm looking for."

"I don't understand, Jack. I thought you loved me."

"So did I."

"But you don't?"

She looked at him. He did not answer.

"Is it because of your book? Is that it?"

"No, that's not it. There'll be other books."

"In Alaska?"

"And other places."

"A lot of other places." She said it not as a question.

He nodded.

"I hope . . ." She smiled. "I hope you find what you're looking for."

"Good-bye, Felicity."

Impulsively, she kissed him. He turned and started to leave.

"Jack."

He looked back.

"Write."

"I intend to." He smiled and walked away.

Soon his step picked up momentum. Charged with energy, he was eager to get moving. To hell with Captain Diequest and all the Captain Diequests of the world. And all the other enemies who tried to beat him down. Poverty, shame, prejudice—the canneries, the mills, the Oakland Street Railroad Power Plant and Peter Pierce, Florence Bambridge, Farnsworth and all connivers and oppressors. He would beat them all.

He made his way into the crowd. Look out—Jack London was coming through.

He heard the call of the *Umatilla*'s shrill whistle. And Jack London heard another call. A distant clarion call that only he could hear—telling him that each man has just so much time. Use it!

And use it he would. Every hour. Every pulsing minute. On land and sea. Never would any man live as much, and write as much, in so short a time. He would ignite a literary revolution. They were all there in his mind and body, begging to be born and to live forever:

Call of the Wild

A Daughter of the Snows

The Sea Wolf

White Fang

The Road—The Iron Heel—White Silence—Cruise of the Dazzler—Martin Eden—Tales of the Fish Patrol—John Barleycorn—South Sea Tales—Adventure—When God Laughs—Smoke Bellew—The Valley of the Moon

. . . and all the rest, written by Jack London, who lived less than forty years and lives forever.

This book may b